Dark Days: Infected

Written by:
Greg Wilburn

Edited by:
Michael Matchell

www.darkdaysinfectedbook.webs.com
This is a work of fiction. All of the characters, organizations, and events portrayed in this work are either products of the author's imagination or are used fictitiously.
Cover Art Drawn by Gregory Wilburn
Cover Art Designed by Michael Matchell
DARK DAYS: INFECTED
ISBN-13: 978-0615876061
ISBN-10: 0615876064

First Edition (revised): August 2013

Printed in the United States of America

0   9   8   7   6   5   4   3   2   1

To Scraps; the best puppy I never had.

CONTENTS

NOTE FROM THE AUTHOR

Thank you so much for purchasing the first edition of my book, *Dark Days: Infected.* I cannot express my excitement and gratitude for your interest in this story! I hope that you enjoy reading my book as much as I enjoyed writing it! I am open to suggestions and guidance as I continue on this journey, so feel free to contact me at: www.darkdaysinfectedbook.webs.com/contact-us with any idea or suggestion you have!

I'd also like to thank Michael Matchell, my Editor and Public Relations Director for all his hard work and dedication! He has been alongside me, guiding me through this process every step of the way!

Most importantly, I'd like to thank my family for their never ending love and support. I would not be where I am today without them.

Huge thanks,
Greg Wilburn
Author

TAPE #1

It all began on a sunny day in March; so close to my birthday too. Why do such bad things have to begin on days with good weather? I remember it like it was yesterday, although it was around four years ago today.

Why am I even doing this? Who would want to remember this tragedy or collect these memories that all I want to do to them is destroy them and forget them forever? But she says I need to do this; that way, all those we have loved and lost will not be forgotten.

Since that's the case, let me start with the beginning of how this hell came to be four years ago.

I used to work as a janitor before the whole world went down in flames. Not that I had always wanted to be one, but when the economy is as bad as it was then, and you've lost your job on top of it, your only option is to take what you can get. Before my days of vomit cleaning and inglorious toilet plunging, I was a lawyer.

I had a firm with three other men I had known in college, and we were decently successful in our endeavors. I had the life, or what you could call living in the middle class standard of living. I had a car, a wife, a kid on the way, and a dog named Scraps.

We called him Scraps because he wouldn't start begging for food at the table until the meal was done and only the scraps of what had been eaten were left. Scraps was an amazing dog. I call him a dog because

1

even though he was only a year and a half old, he acted very maturely. I could always depend on him to brighten my day. He took quickly to doggy training, the usual, you know; not to pee on the couch or to poop in my bed at three in the morning because he was afraid of raccoons. I remember one incident that occurred just a few weeks before the outbreak.

I walked into the house we had foreclosed the week before to the sound of running water. That was weird because no one had been home. My wife was at the doctor to check on the baby to make sure we were coming along nicely and I had just come back from work. The only person who could have turned on that water was Scraps. I walked into the kitchen expecting him to have simply turned a faucet or spilled a water bottle over, but to my surprise I turned the corner to find good ol' Scraps peeing into my favorite cookie jar. That set back our training a couple of years for sure. I guess it was my fault in the end because it was shaped like a fire hydrant.

I'll always remember that, not only because Scraps was such a great dog, but mostly because it was one of the few moments of happiness I felt before I lost absolutely everything I loved and cherished.

Sorry for taking so much time to talk about a dog, but he means so much to me when I reflect on him now. Now I feel that I have to introduce the rest of my family. This may take a moment.

I can't express with words how much I loved them, and now how much I miss them, but I will do my best to paint a picture of the most beautiful woman in the world and the heavenly child we would have had if all of this hadn't happened.

She was, and still is, the love of my life. I met her in high school. I was a hard working student who happened to be the captain of the wrestling team and a good guy in general. I was well-liked by those around me because not only was I smart, but I actually had a personality.

However, that doesn't compare to her. I think I was in love from the first moment I saw her. She was new to the school my senior year, and to this day I have never seen a creature more beautiful. I was walking to my Principles of Physical Science class when I happened to look over my shoulder to see her. She was gorgeous.

She had sandy blonde hair and the face of an angel. Her body had an athletic build that was shaped by all the gymnastics she did as a child and her cross country running she did all the time. She had the body of a goddess that was tempered underneath her more conservative clothes. I never once saw her wear anything too revealing, and I respect her for treating herself with such care and dignity.

She wore deep blue jeans that made her bright red shoes seem to bud as roses do in early spring. She had a slate gray shirt on that fit her snugly, but not like a glove. You could tell that she was hiding herself a little underneath through the way she did not reveal too much like other girls I always saw around school. Those things did not catch my attention as much as her eyes did.

When I saw those blue-green eyes twinkle in the sunlight, all I could imagine was the meeting between the earth and the sea that you always find in landscape pictures of faraway places that people rarely frequent. The way the rocks covered in vegetation meet the crashing sea shows how such natural majesty meets such undiscovered beauty. I can never forget how those innocent eyes pierced my soul and seemed to tell me of an untold beauty I had never experienced in this world.

A week went by when I would just glance up at her and keep my distance so I wouldn't seem too interested in her. Only once did our eyes meet. I remember it clearly. It was Tuesday morning around break when I happened to catch her eyes.

At first it seemed surreal as I gazed into those lovely eyes, and then all of a sudden her expression changed. Her face changed from one of intrigue and interest to a contortion of surprise with a hint of disgust. I had looked a little too long and from then on I convinced myself not to look at her anymore for fear of having a restraining order placed on me.

As luck would have it, she ended up in my class a week later because her schedule had been messed up at the beginning of the academic year. I think that was what started our relationship.

Maybe not that; when I really think about it, our relationship started when I went up to her and said hello and she immediately blurted out in the middle of class, "Hey! You're that guy who kept staring at me across the quad! Nice to meet you!"

That kept me at bay for a few weeks.

After my shame and embarrassment subsided, I was able to get to know her through our discussion group in class. We became friends instantly; and when I say we became friends, that's all that I mean. At least from her side of things. I saw her as the most beautiful woman in the world, but she only saw me as a dorky guy who wrestled with sweaty men on a mat because I still didn't want to admit I was a flamboyant homosexual. Over my senior year we became great friends and spent a lot of time with each other. We graduated from high school and kept in touch all summer. I would drive out to her house at least three times a week to visit her and her family. I took her on multiple outings, which I would consider dates, but she considered them to be friendly outings.

After summer, college is where our relationship began to change. I went to the local university while she took her first year off in order to travel around the country as an intern for a national women's organization. She told me that it helped empower women to be all that they could be in the world around them.

We kept in touch all that year and were as close as ever when she returned home to attend the same university I was attending. I was studying pre-law and she began to study for a career as a first grade teacher because that had always been her dream.

During our junior year of college, our relationship changed. One night, as we sat on the porch of her house on her favorite tire swing, she confessed her feelings for me. I confessed mine, and to her surprise, I had liked her from the first day I ever laid eyes on her. That was the beginning of change in our lives, and little did I know, it would be the beginning of the end.

TAPE #2

We continued to date through the last two years of college. After that, I had the unbelievable privilege of making her my wife. We had the wedding five months after my proposal in the local chapel. We had a simple wedding; she always said the simple things are what mattered most to her.

After that, she received her teaching credential and went back to her hometown to teach first graders in the local schools. I continued with my education in law and began to attend law school. It was rough for the first two years, but with her as my foundation and support, combined with my desire to succeed and reach my dreams, we made it through.

During my final year of law school, and our fourth year of marriage, we found out we were going to have a baby. We were so excited, and she was the most excited of all. That is where Scraps comes into the picture.

Before our dreams of parenthood were fulfilled, I bought her a little puppy because her baby fever was so intense. Not that I minded though, because I was excited at the notion as well. We treated Scraps like our very own child. He made a good replacement, especially when he caused trouble at home.

At this point, the baby was only a fetus and still growing inside my lovely wife. We were on the verge of discovering if we were going to have a boy or girl when it all started to happen.

I'm sorry, give me a moment. This is where the hard part comes in...........

Around the same time that we had the idea of a child introduced into our lives, they talked about a new disease that had recently been discovered in remote areas of Tanzania. I only caught a glimpse of a few of these reports, but from what I saw, it was pretty serious.

People were dying everywhere and there were various reports of people eating one another. I did see a picture of one of the major suspects:

He was a man, about thirty years of age, and all of his pictures featured him in a lab coat. They said he adapted this disease from animal testing and began illegal human testing with it. He captured a group of locals and underwent experimentation. That was not where the danger truly lied; it became a hazard to society, and later to the world, when one of the test subjects escaped into a large city nearby.

The disease spread like wildfire. Over the next few weeks more and more reports were coming out about the disease and what it did to people once it got ahold of them.

One night, as my wife was putting Scraps to sleep in his little doggy bed, I saw the most disturbing report up to that point. Tanzania, along with all of its surrounding countries, were being evacuated. Various videos featured on the report showed empty streets full of chaos and destruction with occasional infected people running about.

It wasn't real to me until I saw a close up of one of the infected. There were both before and after pictures of a little girl that looked to be about ten years of age. Her before picture featured a lovely looking girl with nice brown hair and green eyes. She was wearing a blue sundress and had a smile of pure joy on her face. I almost want to vomit thinking about how the disease ravaged her body, transforming her into a hideous creation beyond comprehension.

The after picture still haunts my dreams to this day. It serves as a reminder of my ignorance, the damage the disease caused to my life and the lives of others, and the loss of hope that I can still feel in my heart like a fresh dagger every single day.

Her skin was solid white, almost as if she was a giant walking ghost.

Her skin was broken in various places where pus and blood were seeping out of her. Her brown hair had turned white in a void of color and was falling out all over her head. Saliva wasn't dripping from her mouth, or if it was, it was a green slime that seemed to cover everything it touched in its filth. She could no longer stand up straight; her posture forced her into a contorted position that gave her a demonic presence in the photo. What scared me the most were her eyes. They had no pupils and were just white with hate and an insatiable desire to feed.

I would go on, but I don't think my stomach could handle it. I think I'm used to it now, but at that time I could imagine no greater evil.

A few weeks later was when the real fear, and my horrible present, came to be. My wife had just gone to our local doctor to go and find out the sex of our baby. It was almost like a birthday to us; we had a cake and a full course meal prepared for when she would return with the good news. We were going to find out first, and then proceed to tell all of our loved ones of the new joy soon to enter the world. I had taken work off that day because absolutely nothing would interfere with the relaying of the fact that I would either have a pretty princess of a girl or a manly brat of a boy.

Clearly, I wanted a girl first. I had always wanted to have a girl first, mostly because I liked to take care of girls. It always made me feel important and needed. I had years of practice caring for the precious jewel of a wife that shone brighter than any diamond I could put on her finger.

I miss that moment of the day, when joy and excitement had completely taken over my senses. I felt numb in the best way possible. I would need to feel that numbness for what would happen that day.

About fifteen minutes after she had gone, I was sitting on the couch, dwelling on the fact that I would soon be a father. I flipped on the television and began to turn through the channels. To my surprise, every single channel I went to was being broadcasted with a news report about the continuing infection. It didn't really catch my attention at first, but after getting to channel three hundred and forty seven, I figured I might as well see what was going on.

It's very interesting how a person's life can be turned completely upside down and destroyed with a simple news report.

The local anchorman did not look his usual professional self. He looked as if he had not bothered to dress up at all that day. Then the report began. I don't really remember much of the report, but I do remember two specific details:

an outbreak had begun in my own hometown not twenty minutes ago. What's worse is the fact that the sentence that followed stated it had begun near the office my wife had gone to see our doctor at.

I panicked. I threw on my coat and jumped into my car. I could only think one thing: I would never let them get to her and I would never let her become the abomination I had seen reported on a few weeks ago.

I sped down the streets. I don't recall how many stop signs I went through or how many red lights I crossed on the way to the hospital entrance. I even smacked the side of the car against a street dumpster taking a sharp turn onto the main road.

However, I never made it to that hospital entrance. Upon entering the main parking lot, I was stopped by a large barrier made of police cars with blaring sirens and various officers holding shotguns. I got out of the car and made a run for the side entrance that was covered by less police force. I was stopped short by a sharp pain against the side of my head.

Next thing I knew, I was being pulled out of a bush by two large officers. They told me that I was not to go in because the infection had spread rapidly and there was little chance of survivors.

I have never begged so much in my life. I begged them to step in and find her. They kept cold stares and said they would never be stupid enough to send in any forces to save a lost cause, let alone a citizen that was likely monster feed by this point in this crisis situation. Still, I begged; I bribed, I cursed, and I threatened until I found my voice hoarse.

I could not believe that they would let the only people I loved above all to sit in that monster den and die like innocent sheep given over to the slaughter. They said they could and would do nothing to help me because they had not received word from the captain to go in yet.

Immediately, I turned to my right and saw a broken window uncovered by the useless police force. I made a run for it. I guess I still had some youth left in me from my days in sports because I saw the officers from before at least seven steps behind me as I dove through the window onto the hospital's main floor. I was in.

I never expected to land in a pool of blood. I never even knew a single person could bleed so much. Through the fractured light let in through the windows of the room I could see the blood before and upon me, as well as the silhouette of the hospital receiving room I had landed in. I picked myself up and walked into the hallway. It was pitch black there, save the occasional ray of light let in through the blinds lining the walls. The stench of death was everywhere; its noxious toxins seeped into my nose and mouth, almost making me vomit at every step.

I made my way down the main hall, going the opposite way of the lighted exit signs at each turn. I knew where to go even in this dark, cold prison. I had been there plenty of times before with my wife as we frequently visited her doctor to keep an eye on her precious cargo. I reconstructed the floor plan in my head: Three hallways, two flights of stairs, and one door at the end of the hallway to come to the office where my wife would be holed up and safe.

I made my way through two of the pitch black hallways when I heard growling behind me. I could see nothing in the dark, but I could feel the evil presence nearby. I turned in the darkness, hoping to see the beast behind me. My eyes searched the dark, but were unable to find anything. I asked the darkness, "Is anyone there?"

What an idiot. It located me immediately. I could feel the tension break as the footsteps rapidly moved in my direction. I ran, with all my might. I ran through the last dark hallway, tripping over what I believed were pillows with a little extra stuffing. I made it up the first flight of stairs and began to ascend up the second. I only made it halfway.

I felt a cold hand grasp my ankle. A chill went through my body grim as Death himself. I fell face first as I was greeted with the taste of cold, hard cement and blood in my mouth.

Behind me, the shriek of a demon pierced the deserted halls of the hospital. I found myself kicking to free myself to no avail.

Finally, after a few strong kicks, I think I managed to kick it in the face somewhere. There was a muffled shriek at the bottom of the stairs as I made my way up and continued to crawl through the hallway leading to the final door. I made it to the door as the creature made another shriek from the stairs below. I pulled myself to my feet at the front of the door. I could still feel blood seeping into my mouth as my tongue felt around. It found teeth missing from the left side as I could still taste the cold cement from my fall a moment ago. I took a deep breath of hope and assurance, turned the knob, and stepped into the waiting room.

I stepped into a room well suited for expectant mothers. Through the dim light in the room I could see that the walls were lined with pictures of babies in all sorts of uniforms and costumes. Like all baby pictures, the babies looked more confused than happy or sad to have pictures taken of them. I knew I would have to put some of those kinds of pictures up in the house later when the baby was born. The floor was carpeted in magazines that advertised the right feeding habits and tools to help the baby learn up to five languages by the time it was three. I locked the waiting room door behind me before going any further.

This room seemed untouched by the evil that lay just beyond that door. Besides the magazines spread out across the floor, everything seemed to be in order. I made my way to the window and opened the blinds. The searing light made its way into the room, banishing the darkness into the remote corners of it. I could see the police down below, guarding the hospital and still refusing to do anything for the innocent people being consumed within it.

I turned my attention back to the office, back to my wife. Just beyond the reception desk would be my wife with the doctor and the news of our impending child. What relief I had felt in that moment.

I walked past the reception desk into the small hallway containing three small waiting rooms. It was surprisingly still there, but I guess they were just keeping quiet in case one of the monsters would be nearby.

Thankfully, they would need to fear no longer; I was there to find them and help them back to safety from the dangers in the hospital.

I opened the nearest door and peeked inside. Nothing there. I walked further down the silent hallway and opened the second door.

I found a woman in scrubs laying face first on the ground in a pool of blood. I walked over to the lifeless body and turned it over. I searched the body to find out who she was. As I expected, it was the receptionist that had sincerely and warmly accepted my wife and I every time we had visited.

Poor woman; she had a series of jagged slashes all the way across her neck. The look of surprise on her face took me aback. It was as if she had not expected to be attacked in her final moments of life.

I couldn't bear it any longer; I closed her eyes, gently placed the body back down, and walked out of the room, shutting the door behind me. I glanced over to the last room, which was not completely closed, but was cracked just a little. My wife would be there, safe and sound.

As I reached for the door, I suddenly found myself stopped, trying to fight my instincts to run away rather than enter into the room where everything I loved was being held safe. Of course, I opened the door to let the light in and see my wife and child unharmed. Nothing prepared me for what I saw next.

The light spread across the room, illuminating the scene where my life was swept away. I saw the doctor first -- or at least what was left of him.

He was face up on the ground, gazing up at me with a blank look of horror and surprise. The floor was covered in blood. I opened the door all the way and saw that he had been torn in half. His intestines were lying all over the floor, covering the ground in a fleshy, bloody maze. Blood was still leaking out of his torso as I found the lower portion of his remains about five feet away, connected by the intestinal maze on the floor.

That's when I heard a shuffling behind the large chair in the room. It could only be my beautiful wife seeing I had come to save her. I called out to the chair, letting her know it was safe to come out and that she would not have to worry anymore. There was a brief silence and then another shuffling noise. Again, I pleaded for her to come out to me so we could escape the hell we had been trapped in.

I said, "It's okay, Honey. I'm here now. I've come to save you and take you home and never let you out of my sight ever again. I'm sorry you had to go through all of this, but it will all be over soon. Trust me."

She stepped out. Namely, it stepped out. It was not my wife behind the chair, but I could still see that it was the woman I had always loved. I took a step back in horror as I could see the disease had taken hold of all that I loved in the world and ripped it out of my life.

Her once gorgeous hair was void of color. Her illustrious skin was torn in various places. I could see pus and blood leaking out of her at the sites of broken skin. She was bent over sideways and had a stature I had only seen in my deepest nightmares. Her eyes broke my heart and pierced my soul. They were no longer a beautiful fusion of majesty and compassion, but now showed a white hate and hunger. In that moment, I could only muster up enough courage to say, "I'm sorry."

She stepped out and dragged her feet in my direction. I staggered back, still muttering apologies that could never find forgiveness. I still remember the shrill cry she let out as she lunged towards me. It pierced my ears and filled the office. It resounded off the walls of the office and the walls of my heart, sobering me to the fact that I had lost everything and it had been entirely my fault.

She landed on top of me, clawing at my throat with desperation and hunger. She was so heavy. Hot, wet tears flew down my face as I begged her to stop while trying to push her away from me. She was screaming at the top of her lungs, revealing her intense desire to feed on my flesh.

I managed to push her to the side of the room closest to the door. I stood up quickly and made a run to the hallway. I got past the receptionist desk and reached the door leading out of the main office. However, I could not make an escape due to the clawing and scratching I heard on the other side of that door.

I immediately knew the creature from before had made its way to the door and was trying to find its way in. I turned around to see the other creature standing in the doorway of the receptionist office, waiting to locate me and make its next attack. More hot tears flew down my face as I no longer saw my love and only saw an abomination that wanted my flesh for lunch. I slid down the wall of the office into a position of defeat. I knelt on the floor, arms wide open. She needed to kill me, she wanted to kill me; I wanted to die.

I closed my eyes as a shrill cry filled the room. Slow, staggered steps got louder with every passing second. I could hear the evil presence getting closer and closer, sensing the easy prey ready to be devoured. All was black.

A gunshot, and the sound of shattering glass. Where did that come from? I opened my eyes.

I saw the hospital waiting room once again, bathed in the sunlight.

The monster was lying next to me on the floor, its face directly beneath mine. I scanned its body in wonder how it had managed to stop. In the middle of its stomach, a gaping hole had been made. More hot tears came to my face as I realized that I had been spared but my wife and child had not. I gazed angrily at the hole in the body of the monster for a moment as it came to full effect: my wife was gone, and now my child had been torn from me completely.

I turned my gaze back to the face of the creature. I could no longer find anything evil about it. Now, in its dying state, I could once again see my wife. She was dying right in front of me.

It was difficult to swallow as she was choking on the blood filling her mouth. There were no pupils in her eyes, but I could sense the fear in her. All I could say was that I was so sorry.

Her eyes searched my face, pleading for help and release. She did not have long left. Her disheveled hand slid weakly across the floor towards me. I reached out and grasped her hand in mine. She was so cold. I looked into the face of my love one last time and more hot tears flew down my bloody face. The last words she heard me say were that I was sorry.

She died, and so did I.

TAPE #3

I heard a muffled gunshot on the other side of the main door. I guess the captain had finally allowed the police to enter the building in search of survivors. I heard one last shriek from the creature from outside, just beyond the door. A gunshot cut through the air, resounding from the other side. I heard a soft moan on the floor and all was silent again.

A few moments passed, and then there was a knock on the door. How polite. Here we were, in the middle of an apocalypse, and someone still had the decency of a human being. "Anyone there?" the voice said.

I replied, "Yeah, I'm right here. Don't shoot; I'm not one of the infected." I heard a sigh of relief on the other side of the door.

"Good, because the sniper outside thought you were a goner. He happened to look through the open blinds to see one of those creatures make its way towards you. It seems he got the shot off just in time. Are you all right?"

I looked down at the child whom I would never know, then into the face of my dead wife. I answered, "No, but I think I'll live." Then he asked me to let him in the room.

I stood up, unlocked the door, and let him in. The officer came in and looked down onto the floor. "Man, talk about a close call. One second late and you would be monster chow. I bet you're glad that

14

thing on the floor didn't get a chance to have its dinner." I said nothing.

He looked at me peculiarly, took a moment, and finally said, "We have to leave right now. There could still be some of the infected around here and I need to get you to safety. Are you ready to go?"

I looked up into his face. He had warmth to him that made me trust him. I took one last look at what was left of my family and said, "Yeah. Let's get the hell out of here."

He led me back through the darkened hospital. I stepped over the creature from the stairs. It looked as if it had once been a boy, no older than sixteen. There was a bullet hole in the middle of its forehead. It had the same look as all the other creatures I had seen: angry and hungry.

We walked back through the hospital in the dark, moving slowly and cautiously. After a few minutes of this, we made it back to the entrance. We stepped out into the daylight and walked into the barricade of police cars with their sirens blaring. I was greeted by a man in a captain's uniform. So this was the captain that refused to help all of the innocent people trapped inside the hospital and thus allowed them to be eaten alive by those monsters.

He was a tall, fat man with a well-trimmed mustache. He wore the uniform with dignity; there was not a dirty spot to be found. His tar black shoes smiled brightly in the sunlight. He proudly bore all of his medals on his uniform to show he was an experienced and capable leader. From my perspective, he was a murderer who let innocent lives be eaten away in the dark hallways of the hospital. He smiled at me proudly and extended his hands towards me for a greeting. I stood there, refusing to return the greeting he had offered.

He placed his hand back at his side and said, "I'm glad to see you made it out all right. Most of the officers have returned to report no survivors. We've hunted down most of the infected running through the halls. Are you all right? You must have gone through quite the ordeal. Do you need anything? Perhaps some food or water?"

I wanted to demand him to bring my family back. I wanted to shout in his face and tell him how all the innocent people that went to the hospital that day were dead because of his ignorance and his decision not to act when they needed help the most. I thought about pushing him to the ground and beating him until he knew the pain I had felt seeing my family die right in front of me.

Instead, I took a moment to recollect myself and said, "No, thank you. I just want to go home." He replied, "That's going to be a problem."

He continued on, "We need to evacuate the city. Some of the infected escaped the hospital and made it into town. The infection is spreading rapidly. There won't be any home to go to."

I had no home, I had no family, I had no hope. I stood there silently, waiting for the captain to tell me what would happen next.

"We have to take you to the quarantine base outside of the city. It's safe there. First, I will need you to be inspected for any bites. If you have any, we are going to have to kill you right here and now. If you're not infected, we'll take you to the base with the other survivors. You will be given safe haven there and not have to worry about any more infected trying to eat you alive. Are you ready?"

I nodded reluctantly and followed him to a nearby ambulance with a doctor inside. He inspected me for any bites. He didn't find any, but he did tell me that I had a dislocated jaw and two broken ribs on my left side from the fall on the stairway. Other than that, I had some minor scrapes and bruises. He helped place my jaw in its proper configuration and bandaged me tightly around the torso. He said I would be fine after I got some rest and food. He sent me back out to the captain with a clean bill of health.

The captain escorted me to a police van and put me inside. I sat in the windowless police van surrounded by guns and other tools police officers use in the line of duty. Beyond that, all I could see was the captain's head. He started the car and off we went.

Although I couldn't see anything, I heard a lot as we drove along. At first, I heard police sirens as we departed from the hospital parking lot. As we drove along the road, I heard numerous shrieks and screams filling the air. There were more creatures out there, looking for people to consume and devour.

At the same time, I never realized the roads through town were so bumpy. I would drive them every day back and forth to work, and they were never this bumpy. I asked the captain what was going on out there.

He told me, "You wouldn't want to see it. The streets are crawling with infected, and whenever they see a moving target, they rush towards it. They're running all about, looking for someone to devour. They've been running into the van for a few minutes now, trying to get at me and you.

Before, I felt bad about hitting them as I made my way through town carrying survivors. Now, I know it sounds a bit sick, but I want to hit every single one of them. You see, my son became an infected yesterday. The news said that the outbreak started today officially, but for me it all started yesterday.

I was building a cabinet in the backyard when it happened. I heard a huge crash in the house, and I instinctively turned towards it to find out what it was. I had a gut feeling to take the hammer I was using, so I grasped it in my hand and carried it into the house with me.

I walked into a completely dead house. I was in the kitchen when he attacked me. He tackled me from behind, knocking me to the floor. I turned to see that my son had become an infected, and his only objective was to eat his dad. The hammer had been knocked from my hand and was on the other side of the island in the middle of the kitchen. My son was glaring at me, daring me to make a move. I broke the silence first.

I threw myself to the other side of the island and grasped my hammer. My son leaped over the island and landed right on top of me. It took one blow to the head to kill him, but I kept on hitting him as he lied limp on the floor. I was crying as I repeatedly bashed his skull with the hammer. After a few minutes, I stopped and threw his body outside. I consoled myself by saying that he was not my son anymore. He was a monster, and in that logic, it's either kill or be killed. After cleaning myself up, I got the call to go into the office. I never told anyone what had happened.

Then the outbreak happened. I sent forces to go out and find survivors. My duty was to collect them and take them to the safe haven that had been established outside of town. The first few trips were hard as I hit a bunch of infected. I kept thinking that they were once human, and that I was hurting innocent people.

After the fourth trip across the city, my mind returned to my son. He hadn't been my son, he was a monster. I was killing monsters, and that is a good thing to do. So, now I want to hit them all. I want to kill all of these monsters that feast on the people we care about and love. I know it's sick, but I have to do this......for my son."

I listened to his story as we made our way to the safe haven. I realized I was not the only one who had lost everything. I hated him a lot less now. My thoughts returned to my family, and I began to understand what he meant.

We sat in silence for the next few minutes. As we drove on, the screams dissipated into the air and could no longer be heard. The road wasn't bumpy anymore. After a few more minutes of driving, we came to a stop. The captain turned around and said, "We're here."

The van doors opened to two rugged looking men and a compound that I recognized as the small army base just outside of town. It was well fortified; There were beige walls at least fifteen feet high laced with barbed wire. There were eight large towers surrounding the compound, and each was stationed with three men holding guns. There were two large buildings that took up much of the compound.

I stepped out of the van and found the captain. He was talking to an older man in an army uniform who looked to be at least fifty. After a moment, the captain turned around and addressed me. He said, "You're here in the safe haven with the other survivors. The army forces here will take good care of you and provide you with protection, food, and shelter. I have to continue to make runs in and out of the city to find more survivors. Thank you for accompanying me and I hope everything will work out for you."

I thanked the captain for his help, and extended my hand towards him for a goodbye. He met my farewell with a firm handshake. He stepped into the van and started the vehicle. He sped out of the open gates at the front of the compound and made a right in the direction of the city. I never saw him again.

TAPE #4

A hand was placed on my shoulder, forcing me to turn around. I locked eyes with the older man that had spoken to the captain. He greeted me with a sarcastic smile and stated, "Please follow me and we will get you some food and rest."

I followed him to one of the large buildings that spanned the compound and stepped inside. I found myself in the main lobby of an office building. It seemed pretty deserted; The floor was neatly covered in camouflaged sleeping bags. Each bag had a pillow, a canteen of water, and a sandwich on top of them. There were two women sitting at a clerk's desk, but besides that, the room was completely empty.

I walked up to the clerk's desk and greeted the women. They warmly greeted me and then asked me to have a seat. I pulled up a chair, waiting for them to begin questioning me. They asked me some routine questions about my age, occupation, marital status, and how I came to be there. After this, one of the women told me to go upstairs to the survivor's floor where I would receive some food and a bed for the night. I thanked them and headed up the flight of stairs leading to the second floor. I treaded carefully up the stairs, reminiscing the fall I had in the hospital that had graciously given me my dislocated jaw and broken ribs.

At the top of the stairs I could see the second floor clearly. It was filled with a sea of people. I scanned the room; the floor was strategically covered in cots to create wide aisles in the room, there were tables on the far side of the room with soldiers standing behind them serving food to people, and all of the windows of the room had been covered up with large sheets of metal. I could pick out a few faces in the crowd, but for the most part I focused on finding some food and rest. I entered the nearest line in an attempt to wait for food. I spent much of my time running my tongue around my mouth, taking the time to feel around on the left side of my face where various gaps were present; No more perfect smile. There was still some blood oozing into my mouth, but it was not a big deal.

After an eternity of waiting, I reached the front of the line. As soon as I stepped forward and asked for some food, a young soldier pulled up a sign that read "Out of Food" and placed it on the table. I looked over to my left, at the other lines spread across the room. Each one was longer than the one I had been in, and I was not willing to wait any longer.

I told myself, "This is ridiculous. Forget about the food and just get some rest. You can always get food in the morning." I made my way to a cot on the far side of the room, away from all the foot traffic. I found a cot that was spread out right up against one of the walls. It had a pillow, a canteen of water, and a blanket. I lied down on the cot and tried to make myself comfortable. I took a drink of water to wash out my mouth, and then proceeded to go to sleep. My stomach growled ferociously, but I tried to ignore it. I closed my eyes and hoped to find sleep.

I awoke the next morning; at least what I believed was the next morning. I woke up in a different room than the one I had fallen asleep in the night before. This room was not widespread and full of people, but this one was small and lonely.

After snapping out of my sleepiness, I glanced around the room. The walls of the room were covered in army recruitment posters and framed pictures of important soldiers receiving recognition. Other than the walls, the room was completely bare. I found myself on a cot, missing my blanket, water, and pillow.

I sat up in a panic. Immediately, my stomach called out to me. The message it sent to my brain made my whole body hurt. I really needed food. I licked my lips, only to find them chapped and bloody. I stood up in a panic. How had I ended up here?

I walked briskly to the door and opened it up. I was greeted by a young nurse as I entered the hallway. She said, "Good evening. I'm glad to see you pulled through all right. You may be wondering why you ended up in that room. Four days ago, you made a huge disturbance in the middle of the night. You were writhing on your bed and screaming nonsense. We had you moved to this smaller room where you couldn't scare any more people."

I looked blankly at her. She continued on: "I believe you were having night terrors based on your experiences from the day you arrived. You can rest now, or, when you're ready, we can go and find you some food and water." I immediately said, "Please, lead the way."

I followed the nurse down two or three empty hallways. We passed a few offices where I could see soldiers shuffling papers and putting information into computers. She led me to the end of the hallway and through two huge, oak doors. I entered through, back into the room I had apparently been removed from four days ago. I saw the sea of people once again filling the room.

My stomach rumbled vigorously in my body, filling my ears. I continued following the nurse through the room. I was led to the front of the nearest food line in order to receive food and water. I gratefully thanked her for her help as she handed me a plate of mashed potatoes, broccoli, and a chicken breast accompanied with a cold canteen of water. She told me to eat up and return to my room to continue to rest when I was finished.

I looked after her as she walked away, disappearing into the sea of people. I spotted a chair on the wall nearby and headed in its direction. I glanced into the faces of people as I headed over; I saw a few angry faces, probably due to the fact I had been able to pass before them in the line. I also saw a few frightened faces, most likely due to the nonsense I had apparently been spouting a few nights earlier. I sat down on the faded wooden chair. I ignored the people walking by, looking in my direction while whispering suspiciously.

I focused on the banquet I held in my hands. I slammed the broccoli down my throat with my fork first. It tasted so fresh and green. Next, I turned my attention to the creamy mashed potatoes. I ate these slowly, savoring their smooth texture.

I stopped to take a large gulp of water from the canteen that was cold to the touch. The water glided down my throat with ease, giving me a cool sensation that spread all throughout my body. I had to take a second gulp, and then a third. By the time I had reached my sixth heaping gulp, my lips found the canteen empty.

There was only one thing to do: I had to finish the plump chicken breast waiting for me on my plate. I used my steel fork to saw the large chicken breast in half. The juices seeped out of the skin and spread across the plate as I cut my way through. I split the chicken down the middle, creating two succulent pieces of chicken ready to be consumed. I pierced the first piece of chicken and threw it down my throat. It was perfectly tender and tasted divine. I pierced the last piece with my fork and began to move it slowly towards my mouth, preparing myself for the climax of my meal.

I was only halfway when I saw her; then my life changed forever.

TAPE #5

I looked up to meet the eyes of a very young girl standing directly in front of me. She was so tiny and beautiful; she looked to be no more than six or seven. This little girl had straight, dark brown hair that fell down to her shoulders. She was very skinny, and it was very apparent underneath the clothes she was wearing.

She was wearing a puffy, purple jacket to keep her warm. Underneath, you could see that she had a faded light blue shirt on. She wore dark blue jeans with some rips in them. They had a hole on the right knee, where one could see she had a scrape that was still bleeding. There were pink shoes on her feet that were covered in large, pink sequins. Those shoes shone like bright stars in the reflected light of the room. She had gorgeous bright green eyes that looked as if the finest jade from the most exotic of places had been placed there. She also had some dirt on her face, which starkly contrasted her pale skin.

She looked directly into my eyes with a deep, sincere smile, and asked, "Excuse me, but can I have some food?" I looked around curiously, trying to spot an oncoming parent that would take her away so I could finish the rest of my meal. I told her, "I'm sorry, but this is my food. If you wait in line with your mommy and daddy you can get something to eat."

She immediately replied, "Mommy got lost in the city; She has to hide at our house until it's safe for her to come here without being hurt by the monsters; my daddy told me. Daddy's been gone for a long time, and I don't know where he is now."

I didn't know what to do. My stomach still groaned, telling me that I needed to eat that succulent piece of chicken on the edge of my fork. Then I heard her little stomach groan intensely right in front of me. I looked into her hungry green eyes for a second, and my heart began to melt in compassion.

I looked up in order to spot a short food line so that I could wait with her to get food. To my surprise, the room had no more lines. The sea of people had dispersed; each individual had returned to their cot in order to eat their meal. I stood up, looking at the nearest food table. There were no soldiers there to serve the food, and the food had been removed as well. The only thing that remained was a large sign that clearly stated, "Out of Food." I quickly scanned the other tables spanning the room, and they all contained the same signs signifying the end of the food rush.

I turned my gaze back to the little girl. Her stomach growled intensely for a second time. I sat back down, defeated. I looked her in the eyes and reluctantly handed her the fork. Her eyes glowed with excitement as I handed my last piece of chicken to her.

She looked down and placed it in her mouth. She chewed meticulously so she would not miss a single bit of flavor that the chicken held for her. She swallowed it slowly, and then returned my gaze with a grateful smile. She happily yipped, "Thanks Mister!"

I asked her what her name was and where her daddy was. She told me how her dad had walked away while talking with one of the soldiers, leaving this poor little girl to fend for herself. I continued to speak with this little girl, asking her various questions.

I learned a lot about her in the few minutes we spent talking. I found out these things: she was six and three quarters years old, her favorite color was green because it made her eyes look even prettier, her favorite food was brownies, she liked to dance, she had a pet frog that died a long time ago, she didn't have any siblings, she played soccer this past summer, she could play the piano, and she was still afraid of the dark unless she could sleep with her favorite teddy bear.

She unzipped her puffy jacket and pulled out a worn teddy bear. It had shaggy fur, buttons for eyes, and a large heart shaped patch sewn onto its stomach. It also had a smile that spread ear to ear on its large, round face.

She told me she had had it since her second birthday. I looked in astonishment at this well preserved bear and thought about how nice it would be to have it there with her every night, watching over her as she slept. After a few more seconds, she stuffed the bear back into her jacket and zipped it up to her chin.

I felt sleep creep up behind my eyelids, making them heavy. I decided it was time for me to go back to my room and try to rest. But what about the girl? I couldn't just leave her there alone. I forced the sleep out of my eyes and asked her, "How about we go look for your daddy?" She excitedly consented.

We walked across the floor, making our way through the maze of cots. We reached the stairway and headed down. We landed on the first floor, where nobody was to be found. We walked across the room and stepped into the cold air outside. It was evening, and one could see the sun setting just beyond the high walls of the base.

I felt a small, cold hand slip its way into my right palm. I looked over to my right, meeting the eyes of the little girl. She had a shy smile on her face. I gave her a nice big smile to calm her and said, "Okay. You stay close to me and we'll go find your daddy."

We began to walk across the compound, over to the second building. There really was no other place for her father to be; the base was only so big. The night air crept through my skin, sending shivers through my entire body. I stopped in my path and took a second to gaze into the sunset declining over the nearest wall. It was a sight to see.

The large half circle creeping behind the wall was a bright yellow color. It illuminated the surrounding sky in a flurry of pink, orange, red, and violet, creating within me a sense of awe that I had never felt before. Could things this beautiful still exist in the midst of all the ugliness happening just beyond the compound walls? I felt the little girl tug at my sleeve, signifying she was ready to move on.

My eyes returned to the building on the other side of the compound. This building was very similar to the building we had just departed from. It stood as a dark entity in the shadow of the setting sun. A few lit windows glowed in the darkness, showing somebody had to be over there for us to talk to. We finished the short walk to the large front doors of the building.

There was a plaque just above the door that read: "Loyalty and Honor. Sacrifice for the sake of the many. This is our creed. Let us live and die to uphold the standard to which we are held." I read the plaque two or three times, trying to understand the true meaning of what the words were trying to say.

How could anyone truly live these words, especially in a world like ours? I could not think of any answers then, but now I can see full well the wealth of answers that lie before me that day.

I turned my gaze back to the large wooden doors of the building. I grabbed the iron latch and opened up the door. We entered into another large office building.

The room was full of cubicles, constructing a maze that needed a navigator if we were every going to find this girl's father. I spotted a woman carrying a stack of papers into one of the nearest cubicles. She would be our best bet.

We walked over to the entrance of the cubicle and peeked inside.

The woman was sitting in a padded armchair, typing on a computer. After a few moments of waiting, she turned around to face us. She looked at me with a warm smile and said, "Excuse me, but can I help you?" I answered, "Yes. We are looking for this girl's father. He has been missing and we need to find him as soon as possible."

She gave me an understanding nod and motioned us to sit in the chairs that stood against the back wall of the cubicle. Once we had taken seats, the woman turned her attention from me to the girl. She asked her routine questions: what her name was, where she was from, what her father's name was, where she last saw him, and various other questions. The girl answered every question quickly and excitedly, maybe in hope of finding her father as soon as possible with her help.

The woman finished questioning her and thanked her for her

cooperation. She turned away to her desk and began to fumble through the drawers. She turned back to the girl and handed her a bright green lollipop. She took it excitedly while belting out a loud "Thank you!"

The woman turned her attention back to me and told me we would need to travel to the second floor of the building to find someone who could help us find the girl's father more quickly. Then she affirmed the girl's hopes by saying, "The base is only so big. We shouldn't have any trouble finding her father." I gratefully thanked her for her assistance before our departure.

I grabbed the little girl's hand in mine and led her out of this cubicle, on through the maze filling the room, and up the stairway on the far side. At the top of the stairs was a large, metallic door that contained a nameplate reading: "Storage." We turned to look at each other, dumbfounded that the woman would send us to a storage room when anyone who could help us was on the floor we had just left. I shrugged my shoulders and hesitantly opened the door.

It opened to the entire second floor of the building, revealing a storage room that had been converted into a makeshift set of offices. On the left side of the room there were some lighted desks where people in uniforms sat. On the right side of the room was a large section where supplies were being stored and stacked on various racks. We stepped in and walked across the blank white floor to the nearest desk. We came up to an older woman sitting at a desk who motioned us to have a seat. We sat in the stiff wooden chairs and waited for her to respond to us again.

I looked down at the little girl, who returned my gaze with a large, green smile. She was twirling the lollipop in her mouth and dyeing her whole mouth green. She pulled it out of her mouth and proudly declared, "It's yummy!" She placed the lollipop back in her mouth and began to wait for the woman's response once again.

After a few minutes of shuffling papers, the woman turned her attention towards us and said, "How can I help you this fine evening?" I took a second to plead my case in order for her to help us find the girl's father. After listening intently to my story, she simply said, "Follow me."

She stood up and motioned us to follow her as she walked away.

We followed her out of the storage room and back down the stairs to the maze of cubicles. We turned a few corners, becoming more and more lost in the maze's depths each time.

Finally, we came to a stop with a man sitting alone in the nearest cubicle. Immediately, the little girl ran into the man's arms while exclaiming, "Daddy! Daddy! We found you!"

After the initial warm embrace with this rugged looking man, she pulled herself away and scolded him. She said harshly, "Why did you leave me alone? You meanie! I was so worried about you! Don't you ever leave me alone ever again!"

It warmed my heart to see that she had finally found her father. I turned and thanked the woman for her help. She took her leave, disappearing behind the nearest corner of the closest cubicle. I turned my attention back to the little girl and her father.

After another scolding, and a few long apologies, the man took her out of his lap and came up to me. He was a small, stocky man with large rimmed glasses. He had specks of gray in his black, glossy hair. I could see his muscles bulging out of the red shirt that was obviously too tight for his build. His face looked hardened, like that of the construction workers I had seen in town. He wore bright blue jeans that were quite faded. He looked at me, gave me a large, toothy smile, and extended his hand towards me. I shook his dry, calloused hand while returning his smile with my own.

He told me, "Thank you so much for looking after my little girl. I thought I had lost her for good. After getting lost in my conversation with the soldier, I looked everywhere for her to no avail. Ultimately, I was sent here to wait until someone found my daughter and brought her back to me. Again, thank you so much!"

I told him no thanks was necessary, that I was just here to help. Still, he was relentless with his gratitude, thanking me again for the deed I had performed. After a brief conversation about the state of things going on outside the walls of the base, I suggested we make our way back to the other building for bedtime.

The father took his little girl by the hand and we attempted to navigate ourselves out of the maze we had been stranded in. I led the way as we continually turned wrong corners, retracing our steps and trying different routes until we ultimately found the front of the building once again. We exited through the doors of the building back into the cool night air outside.

We walked across the compound in silence, gazing up at the bright stars now spanning the wide expanse of the sky. I had never been much of a star gazer, but that night the stars seemed to shine brighter as they smiled down on the three of us. We watched the stars until we made it back to the front doors of the compound's first building.

We entered the lobby and immediately made our way up the stairs just in time to hear a nearby soldier exclaim, "Lights out in ten minutes! Make sure to find your way to your cots and get settled for the night!"

I led the way back to the wooden chair I had sat in when I had met the little girl. When we reached the chair, the father said, "Good. Nobody's taken our cots. Good night's sleep coming up!" At the mention of sleep, my eyelids began to get heavy. My body became lethargic, reminding me how badly I needed to return to the sleep I had given up in order to help the little girl.

I sat down in the chair to make sure the man and his daughter got settled before heading back to my little room in the hallways of the building. The man picked up his daughter and placed her on the cot across from me. He pulled the blankets up to her chin and gave her a kiss on the forehead. He began to step away when her little hand grasped his pant leg.

He turned back to his daughter as she said, "Will you still be here? You promise not to leave again?" He replied, "Of course, sweetie. I won't ever leave your side again. Now get some sleep." She turned over and began to snore before the man reached the other side of the aisle to talk to me.

He sat down on the floor next to me, his sturdy back supporting him against the wall. He gazed off in the direction of his daughter. After a few moments, he said aloud, "It's been hard on her since her mother went missing. I had to tell her that she was safe so she wouldn't get alarmed. Now, I don't know what to tell her. I know in my heart that my wife is gone. I can feel it in my soul. It's like a rubber band that's stretched until it breaks. I held onto the lie that she was okay as long as I could, but I know without a shadow of a doubt she's either dead or one of those monsters running about the streets of town.

Either way, I've lost her. We've lost her. The rubber band has snapped, and I can tell you, it hurts more than I ever thought possible. I have to tell her that her mother is still okay because I can't bear to see that innocent little girl go through any more pain."

My thoughts turned to my own family. I knew he was doing the right thing by hiding this from his daughter. If only I could hide things like that from myself. I wished I was naïve enough to believe my wife and child were still alive. I wanted desperately to live with the vain hope that everything would be okay, to feel life flow within my heart again.

I put my hand to the left side of my chest, making sure I still had a pulse. I could feel my heartbeat fueling my body, but inside myself I knew I no longer had a heart. All that remained was a black hole full of regret and failure.

Tears began to well up in my eyes as I tried to hold them back. I managed to take control of myself enough to tell him, "You're doing the right thing. Don't let her experience that kind of pain. It's too much at her age.

I think I better go and get some rest. I will come back and find you guys in the morning. Have a good night."

The man looked up at me and gave me a nod of approval. I didn't wait for him to get up. I turned away and made it through the labyrinth cots, to the nearest wall where I had entered the room with the kind nurse from before. I stepped through the large doors and began to walk down the hallway.

Tears began to flow down my face, creating small clear rivulets in my dirty, unclean skin. I found my room and stepped in. I closed the door and locked it behind me. I sat down on my empty cot.

I looked around the room at the posters and pictures of the soldiers surrounding me. They were laughing at me, mocking my failure to protect all that I had loved in the world. My mind raced, telling me it was entirely my fault. Heaping sobs racked my body, making my whole being shake; It hurt everywhere. My mind was pounding as my whole body heaved in a deep, inconsolable grief.

I don't know how long I cried, but the sobs were the last thing I remember before I woke up to the scream.

TAPE #6

At first I thought it was a dream. I sat up in my bed, dizzy from the energy expended earlier. A shrill scream filled the air, cutting through the dense silence of the hallway.

I became alert in an instant; the scream had sounded just like the ones I had heard before in the hospital. I stood up next to my cot, waiting to hear anything else.

There was a slight scratching noise in the hallway. As I stood there in the darkness, it grew in intensity. Whatever it was, it was making its way down the hall, right past my door. The scratching noise sent sharp chills down my spine as it slowly passed by. After a few moments, everything was silent again. Two loud gunshots filled the air. Then the panic began.

I reacted immediately; I threw the door open and stepped into the hallway. The lights of the hallway flickered on, blinding and disorienting me for a second. Once my eyes had adjusted to the new light, I could see the scene clearly.

Blood covered the floor in thick, red ooze. I looked over to my right first. I saw a young, frightened soldier holding a smoking silver pistol. He had a look of utter horror on his face. His arms and legs shook visibly. He screamed at me in a cracked voice, "You have to get out of here! They're everywhere! Run! Run!" I never got to give him a reply because as soon as he had barked his orders, he took off running around the

32

corner behind him. I turned to my left to see what he had shot in the lonely corridors of the building.

I saw a jumbled and twisted corpse on the bloody floor, one of its gnarled arms reaching towards the end of the hallway that led towards the large room where the rest of the survivors would be. I stood there for a second to take in the scene. Then I walked in the direction of the corpse. I came up next to the body and knelt down beside it.

It was definitely one of the infected. The body had become gnarled and tangled as the disease had clearly ravaged the body of this woman. She had cuts all over her arms and legs, which were filling with blood and pus. She was face down on the floor, and I could see a puddle of thick, green spittle mixed with the blood spreading from her head.

My mind immediately flashed back to the father and the little girl just beyond the doors. I needed to make sure they were okay. I ran through the empty halls of the building until I came back to the large wooden doors that led into the room with the sea of people. I placed my hand on the handle of the closest door and began to push it open. I stopped halfway as a thought occurred to me. What if there were other creatures lurking around this floor? I had to be careful. I had the impending feeling that something was going on around here.

I opened the rest of the door to a grim scene. The room that had once contained a sea of people was completely empty, save a slew of bodies lying all over the ground. The walls were covered in streams of thick, red blood. Everything was in disarray. The cots were thrown about and remnants of food and water canteens were to be found everywhere underneath overturned tables.

I began to walk around the floor, examining the bodies thrown about. It was a mix of human and infected bodies. The human bodies had slashes across their necks, arms, and legs. Some had gunshots in them, signifying the confusion that had taken place sometime earlier. The bodies of the infected were like that of the body left in the hallway. I glanced over their bodies, looking at the disgusting abominations those people had become.

They all shared the same characteristics: They had no pupils, their hair was beginning to recede from their scalps, their skin was breaking in various places, blood was beginning to seep through their broken skin, their posture was gnarled and twisted, and they had expressions of insatiable hunger on their faces.

I navigated my way through the room, scanning each body in the fear that the father and his daughter were either dead or had become the abominations covering the floor. I heaved a sigh of relief when I finished looking at the last body on the floor, realizing that they were either in another part of the compound, unhurt, or had somehow completely escaped from the monsters running about.

I turned behind me, looking for something to protect myself with. There was no way I was going to go outside without a weapon. I began to retrace my steps, looking for anything I could use as a means of protection. Near one of the overturned food tables I could see a metal bar the length of my arm. It was lying in a pool of blood near the base of the nearest leg. I grasped it in my hands and felt the heavy weight of the metal. I grabbed a nearby jacket on the floor and used it to cleanse the bar of the blood stuck to it. I threw the jacket on the ground and made my way to the stairway leading to the floor below.

The lights were on downstairs, revealing a trail of blood leading from where I was to the main floor. I grasped the bar tightly, holding it in front of my body like a sword. I took slow, cautious steps down the stairs. I watched my surroundings carefully as I made my descent, making sure I would not be taken by surprise by any creature that could be lurking about. I reached the base of the stairs and saw the first floor in full view.

The same horrid scene I had seen on the second floor was repeated there on the first. However, instead of civilian bodies, soldiers' bodies lined the floor alongside those of the dead infected. Those soldiers had to have been taken by surprise because there were no guns to be found on the entire floor. I began to make my way through the field of bodies, checking for anything useful to take with me as I departed.

One of the infected had a large knife in its skull, which I pulled out and tucked into my belt. I found an army backpack on the floor, which I emptied and carried with me as I continued to scavenge on the floor. I found a full canteen of water, some power bars, a flare, and some army food packages.

After scavenging for a few more moments, I placed the gathered items in the backpack and put it on. I took the metal bar back into my hands and made my way to the main doors of the building. I took a deep breath, opened the door, and stepped outside.

The compound was a very grizzly scene to behold. Bodies were all across the compound, seeming to make a path from the building I was at to the building on the other side of the compound. The main gates of the base were open, most likely because some had tried to escape the infection that had gotten into the compound. I could see a few army cars still idling by, patiently waiting for a driver to step in and get them off of the base. I began to step towards the nearest car when cries filled my ears.

I turned to see two dark, twisted silhouettes on the far side of the building, waiting to spot a moving target. I gauged the situation in my mind: I could attempt to get through the infected and enter the car unscathed, or I could make a run to the building on the far side of the compound where there were no infected to be seen. I decided to make a run for the building.

I immediately broke out in a sprint towards the building. More cries filled the air as the silhouettes moved quickly after me. I could sense them moving in on me, getting closer with every step I took. I had to lose weight.

With one powerful thrust, I threw the backpack from me in the direction of the monsters. I still held onto the metal bar, just in case I didn't make it to the doors in time. I made my way across the compound and reached the large doors. I threw the door open and slammed it behind me. I held the door closed and locked it. After locking the door, I could hear the cries of the infected right outside. They began to bang on the door, desperate to enter the building. I took a step back and held the bar tightly against my chest.

That was when I realized I was completely in the dark. I felt my way to the nearest wall and began to search it for a light switch. I moved slowly along the wall, making sure not to make too much noise. I continued to feel along the wall until I found a light switch panel. I flipped all of the switches on, filling the room with blinding white light. I could see the maze of cubicles from the search for the little girl's father. I could still hear the creatures outside attempting to get inside where I was.

I decided to make my way through the cubicles up to the storage room from before. I clutched the bar tightly and began to make my way through. I slid my feet slowly and carefully, checking every corner twice for any creatures. I passed by various offices, finding bodies and blood in some as I passed. I managed to make my way through the maze unheeded by anyone or anything. I reached the stairs leading up to the storage room that had been converted into an office space. I made my way up the steps, still watching my back for any enemies.

I reached the door reading "Storage", and quietly opened it. The room was not as devastated as the other rooms I had seen. There were papers blowing across the floor, but other than that, there seemed to be no disturbances. I spotted the shelves on the right side of the room; there were opened boxes lining the shelves, and I decided to see what I could scavenge from whatever was left.

I walked over to the racks and began my search, going from box to box to find anything useful. When I had reached the third or fourth rack, I saw a large box begin to move in the far corner of the room. I grasped the metal bar in my hand, holding it above my head. I walked cautiously towards the box, ready to swing at whatever sprung forth from it. I made my way to the box, which began to shake intensely as I neared it. I grabbed the top of the box and pulled it quickly away from its spot, metal bar in hand.

I was ready to swing when I heard a small voice cry, "No! Stop! Please don't hurt me!" It was the little girl, trembling with fright. Large tears filled her pretty green eyes, causing me to drop the bar to the ground and bring her into my arms. She wrapped her arms around my neck and said in my ear, "Daddy left to help, but he hasn't come back! I've been here for a long time, and I'm scared Daddy's hurt! I heard screaming outside a while ago, but it's stopped now. Can you help me find Daddy?"

My mind immediately jumped to the conclusion that her father had either become an infected or one of the corpses lying about the compound, but I had to give this scared little girl some hope.

I told her, "Don't worry. We're going to find your daddy and get out of here. Let's get going."

I put the little girl down and stood up. I gave her a big smile of confidence and held my hand out to her. She placed her cold, wet hand in mine and looked up at me to give me a hopeful smile. We made our way through the racks of boxes, hoping to find anything. To my disappointment, all of the boxes I searched through were empty.

The little girl was on her knees pulling a small box from underneath one of the nearby racks. I went down and kneeled next her and asked, "Did you find anything?" She said, "I found this box hiding from me over here. Let's look inside."

The little girl seemed a lot braver and less scared now. She was not crying anymore, and was able to calmly smile up at me. That comforted me, because I was still worried about the creatures outside and her missing father.

I knelt next to her on the floor and helped her open the small box. To our surprise, we found the box to be full of gummy bear packages. That made me laugh cynically. I was expecting something useful, but we got gummy bears instead.

The girl reached in and pulled a package out. She tore it open at the seams and proceeded to eat the candies inside. She looked up at me with a big smile and said, "Yummy! Do you want some?" I shook my head and told her I wasn't very hungry. She finished the gummy bears and said we should take some with us. I consented to having her stick a package in her jacket and putting two or three of them into my own pockets.

After stuffing them in my pockets, I stood up and told the little girl, "Okay. We have to get going. We're going to go outside and look for your daddy. When we go downstairs you need to stay close to me and do exactly what I tell you to do. Okay?" She replied with a silent nod of her head as she stood up in front of me. She grabbed my hand in hers and said, "Okay. Let's go."

I walked with her back to the metal bar I had dropped and picked it back up with my right hand. Then we made our way to the door. I opened the door slowly. Everything was dead quiet. I could see the stairs and the beginning of the maze of cubicles. We made our way down the stairs slowly, watching carefully for any movement. We reached the base of the stairs safely and began to proceed through the cubicles.

When we had turned the second corner of the maze, I heard a shuffling noise somewhere behind us. We stopped in our tracks, listening for any more movement. We seemed to be waiting for an eternity. The little girl began to tug on my arm aggressively. I slowly turned my head to look around.

I turned to see an infected standing at the end of the aisle behind us. It wasn't moving; it was waiting for more movement, just like we were. I had to make up my mind to do something. I began to slide my left foot forward along the floor, making as little noise as possible. The creature still heard me.

It turned its head, and I could see its white eyes widen and its nostrils flare. The expression on its face changed from one of curiosity to one of hunger as it turned in our direction. It began to charge at us, its screams filling the air. I grabbed the little girl and yelled, "Run!"

We turned the nearest corner and sprinted down the aisle. After turning another corner, we ducked into the nearest cubicle. I placed the little girl underneath the desk there and told her to stay put until I got back. She pulled herself into the dark shadow underneath the desk, almost disappearing completely.

I turned around and entered back into the aisle. The creature entered the aisle as soon as I stepped out. I ran in the opposite direction of the monster and turned the nearest corner. I stepped into the nearest cubicle and prepared to strike with the metal bar in my hand. I could gauge where the creature was because its screams still cut through the air. I prepared to swing as I could hear it getting closer and closer. It turned the corner and I swung with all of my might.

I missed. The monster had ducked as it ran past me. It stopped in its tracks and turned to face me. Green spittle was dripping from its gaping mouth. I got the bar ready for a second swing. The monster sprinted towards me, leaping in the air above me. I closed my eyes and swung.

When I opened my eyes, I was lying on the floor. The monster was a few feet behind me, lying on the ground. I could see the metal bar stuck in its ribcage, and a pool of blood was beginning to spread on the floor. I got up and walked over to the creature. As I neared it, it began to twitch. The creature was dying, but it surely wasn't dead. I pulled the knife out of my belt and prepared to slit its throat. As I reached down to grab its head, I heard a loud scream fill the room.

My mind immediately recalled the little girl I had left. I left the dying creature lying there as I sprinted down the aisle, knife in hand. I returned back to where I had placed the girl, but she wasn't there. A cold sweat came over me, as did all the worst case scenarios of what could be happening to her at that moment. Another desperate cry reached my ears.

I turned and ran down multiple aisles, losing myself at every turn. I ran hard, calling out her name and hoping to find her at every turn I took. I finally began to hear her voice clearly. I heard her saying, "No! Please Daddy! No!"

I sprinted down the aisle and turned the corner. I saw the little girl backed up against a wall of the building, seeming to grow smaller and smaller with every passing second. Another abomination was caught in between us, keeping me from getting to her. The abomination had a broken leg that it was dragging alongside it. Yet it was rapidly sliding its presence across the aisle, inching closer and closer to the girl. I yelled out at the creature, trying to draw its attention. I was horrified when it turned around.

It was the girl's father; he had become an infected. Like the other infected I had beheld, the disease made him a new and grotesque creation. It was difficult to look at.

He turned back in the direction of the girl and was almost on the verge of reaching her. The little girl was still crying aloud, pleading with her father not to hurt her. I stood there, stunned. I watched him move in on her, stretching out one of his disheveled hands towards her throat.

I got my wits and started to run with all my might in the direction of this monster. I sprinted down the aisle and leaped in the air, flying directly into him. I tackled him right into the wall and smashed his head against it. Blood and slime flew from his head as he let out a blood-curdling scream. The little girl moved herself away from our fight, scooting herself against the wall of the nearest cubicle.

Even though he was weakened, the monster still had immense strength. He threw me from on top of itself, causing me to land some distance away. Then he leapt up and sprinted in my direction.

He caught me before I could get up. The monster flew into me, picking me up and tackling me through a cubicle and into the next one over. I was dazed. I could only hear the pounding of my heart and the screams of the little girl telling her infected father to stop hurting me.

He pinned me down on a pile of debris and let his cold, horrible spittle drip onto my face. He looked as if he was smiling at me, savoring the meal he was about to enjoy. His sick, demented smile struck fear into my body, causing me to panic and struggle.

I looked to my right, seeing my knife just out of reach. I looked back into the white, evil eyes of my enemy, and his head was getting closer to mine, preparing to take a bite right out of my neck. I continued to panic, seeing the end in sight.

Then, the little girl jumped on the back of the monster and reached for his face. She stuck her thumbs right into his soulless eyes, gouging them and causing fluid to leak from his eyes onto my face. The monster reared up, throwing the little girl from his back and loosening his grip on me.

I reached for my knife and grasped it. I sat up, knife in hand, and plunged it in the middle of his chest. This only knocked him back, allowing me to be on top again. I centered myself, pulled the knife from his chest, and made one huge stab right into his head. Blood spurted out of his head, landing all over the ground and my face.

The smile on the monster's face faded as the life left his body. I pulled the knife out of his head and tucked it back into my belt. The little girl was not far off, crying on the floor. I knelt beside her and placed my hand on her shoulder. She was crying intensely, consoling herself as she said, "He had to do it Daddy...........you were being such a meanie."

I sat down next to her and let her cry for a few more moments. I rested my head against the wall and looked up into the light above me.

This girl had just lost everything, just like I had. I hated myself because I had to be the one who took the last hope this little girl had left in the world. I wiped the blood and tears off of my face and stood up. She was still crying.

I picked her up into my arms, and she put her arms around my neck. She said in my ear, "You won't become a meanie like Daddy, will you?"

I whispered calmly in her ear, affirming that I would never let that happen or leave her alone. I carried her in my arms away from the body of her dead father, disappearing around the corner closest to us. I carried her all the way back to the main entrance of the building. That was the only way out of the hell we were in. There was no scratching or banging on the doors in front of us. I pulled the knife from my belt and clutched it tightly in my hand. I whispered in the little girl's ear, saying, "Hold on tight, we're getting out of here."

I unlocked the door and opened it slowly. There was no life outside in the compound. Perhaps the creatures from before had found better prey. I made my way completely outside, the little girl still in my arms. I took slow, careful steps as I crossed the compound, making little noise. I reached the backpack I had dropped before and slung it over my shoulder.

A car was still idling nearby, waiting for me to drive it out of there. I opened the door of the car silently, and placed the girl in the passenger's seat. I placed the backpack at her feet and got in the car. I locked the doors of the car and looked over at the little girl. She had a crushed look on her face, almost as if all the life had been drained from her body. I decided not to say anything.

I put my foot on the gas and drove us off the compound. I turned left, leading away from the city and the base. I looked back, watching the base disappear until it was only a speck off in the distance.

TAPE #7

I drove through the night, trying to put as much distance between us and the city as possible. Thankfully, we had a full gas tank.

As I drove, I repeatedly glanced over at the little girl. She fell asleep after a couple minutes of driving, laying the seat back and curling up into a small ball within the seat. I felt sorry for this little girl. She was so young, and yet she had to experience so much pain within the past few days.

I remembered the gummy bears I had tucked away in my pockets. I pulled them out and put them on the floor beside the backpack. I would offer them to her later, trying to take her mind off of the loss of her father.

I began to contemplate all that had happened over the past few days. My thoughts would occasionally drift to my wife. I missed her. I touched my chest with my left hand, feeling the piece of my heart that was no longer there. I looked back over at the little girl sleeping in the seat next to me. I thought of the child I would never know. I began to feel like a failure.

Everyone I had met was either dead or a monster running around trying to kill people. The world was going to hell around me, and I was absolutely powerless to stop it. I tried to shake these morbid thoughts as dawn approached. I would see more clearly then.

The sun began to illuminate the landscape around us, revealing a forest of trees in all directions. I continued to drive on, making our way through the countryside. We passed through small towns that were crawling with infected. I plowed right through them, not even batting an eye as I ran those monsters over.

I was beginning to understand what the captain had told me days earlier. The words reverberated in my mind; "It's either kill or be killed...He wasn't my son anymore, he was a monster."

The little girl slept through it all, occasionally shifting her position to make herself more comfortable. I drove until the gas tank was almost empty. As the sun began to set on the horizon, we reached a local highway leading out of the state. I was continuing to drive along when I heard someone calling out to us. I kept moving closer to the voice.

I passed a few cars when I came across a group of six people. Five of them were holding guns. The woman with them was waving her hands, trying to flag me down. I came to a stop right in front of her. The men with her remained in their positions, pointing their guns right at me. She stepped away from the group and walked up to the side of the car. I rolled down the window and could see her clearly.

She was a young woman, probably around twenty years old. She had long red hair that went down to her waist. Her eyes were a deep blue that reminded me of a cloudless sky on a perfect day. She had an athletic build that gave her a demanding presence.

She looked up at me with a contemptuous smile as she said, "State your business here. This is our turf." I replied, "I'm just trying to pass through. We came from back that way, not too far away, and we're just trying to escape all of the infected running about." She said, "If that's so, then why are you driving a military vehicle? There aren't very many of those around here, let alone military bases."

I turned the engine of the vehicle off and took my hands from the wheel. I grabbed the door handle and attempted to exit the vehicle. The woman kicked the door shut, crushing my hand. She pulled out a black pistol and aimed it right at the middle of my head. "No sudden moves!" she shouted.

I clenched my hand in pain and growled in her direction. She barked, "You still have some explaining to do. How did you get here and how did you acquire that vehicle? Explain yourself right now!"

The little girl had woken up because of her yelling. She tugged on my sleeve, causing me to turn to face her. She looked up at me with curious eyes and asked, "What's going on?" I told her not to worry; I just had to talk to these people so we could keep going.

The woman yelled through the open window, "Hey! I'm still over here! Answer me or I'll shoot!" I turned back to face the red-haired woman and explained myself. I only told her about the army base; I left out everything prior to that. After hearing my tale, she placed the pistol back in her belt and opened the door, allowing me to step out. She waved the men over to where we were standing.

I looked back at the little girl in the passenger's seat. She had a worried look on her face and was very quiet as she sat in the seat. The men came over and stopped pointing their guns in my direction. The woman told me, "Sorry, we just couldn't be too careful. We've had a few run-ins with some shady characters."

I told her there was no need to worry; I was not a shady character at all. She smiled, and then asked me where I was going and why. I told her all I wanted to do was get as far away from the city as possible. I wanted to keep the little girl with me safe because she had lost her father and had nobody left.

The woman looked at me and said, "You can't keep going on this highway. About fifty miles away is a military blockade that had been set up a few days before the outbreak. The blockade was taken over by infected a day or two ago, and now it's a festering ground for them. It's not safe at all." I told her, "Either way, I need to find a place to go or stay. I'm almost out of gas and have few supplies."

A wry smile spread across the woman's face as she said, "You can come with us. If you do, just remember that it won't be for free." I took a moment to try to understand what she had said. I looked down at my feet and then at the little girl in the car. There really wasn't much of a choice; we had to go with these people.

I turned my attention back to the woman. I nodded at her and thanked her for allowing us on. She began to walk away as she said, "Okay. Follow me. Boys, keep an eye on this one."

The men watched me as I lifted the little girl from the car. I grabbed the supplies from the car and placed them in the backpack. I put the backpack on my weary shoulders and picked up the little girl in my arms. The girl whispered in my ear, "Where are we going? I'm scared." I told her, "I don't know where we're going, but we have to trust these people. Don't worry, I'll make sure they don't hurt you." The little girl leaned back, giving me an assuring smile. One of the men ushered me into the midst of the other four men and led us into the forest on the side of the highway.

We walked through the dense forest for hours. The last remnants of sunlight crept through the thick trees, elongating the shadows of the forest. The forest took on an eerie feel as we trekked through. All I could hear was the crunching of the leaves underneath our feet and the occasional hoot of an owl nearby. I felt a lot safer in the midst of the armed gunmen. The little girl held on to me tightly, revealing her uneasiness in the dense forest.

After a while, the sun had gone down completely, filling the forest with thick darkness. The men surrounding me pulled out high powered flashlights that brought some security in the unknown blackness around us. A howl filled the air, sending a chill down my spine. I wanted to get out of the forest as soon as possible.

My mind began to wander. Not only did I think of the animals that could be out there, but I began to think of the possibility of an infected lurking about the woods, looking for a meal.

As soon as that thought crossed my mind, a twig snapped loudly right behind us. A cold sweat came over me as we stopped. The little girl clutched my neck frantically, almost choking me to death. Fear crept over me as one of the men turned his flashlight on the ground behind us.

A small rabbit was sitting on the ground, right next to a nearby tree. The full force of the light hit it square in the face, causing it to turn tail and run back into the blackness. The girl loosened her grip on my neck as I let out a deep sigh of relief. One of the men chuckled loudly and said, "What a pussy" underneath his breath. I gave the man a dirty look when he turned back around. The little girl saw this and let out a small giggle.

We turned our attention forward and continued to walk on. After some more walking through the darkness, we came to a clearing with a stream. I could see the whole sky filled with bright stars amidst the tall grass. It was almost as if I could have traced each individual line in the sky, connecting each star and creating a brilliant web in the sky.

We made our way through the tall grass and stopped at a stream. We turned right at its banks and followed it upstream for another period of time. I continually glanced up at the stars as we walked. I looked in my arms to see the little girl gazing at the stars in the sky too. She looked calm and peaceful there in my arms.

The stream led us through another patch of dark forest which broke out into another large clearing. Under the light of the stars I could see our destination.

In the middle of the clearing was a large house that looked like a mansion. It was surrounded by a tall brick wall that contained two sets of thick, steel doors. There were two entrances into the fortress, one on each side of the property.

We came up to the doors and waited for a few moments. Some large men pushed open the steel doors, revealing more of the house. The men with guns led the way into this large fortress. We entered the grounds and came face to face with the red-haired woman once again. The light of the stars lit up her face, giving her an angelic glow. I turned my head around to see the steel doors close behind us, locking us in the enclosed space.

The woman walked towards the group. The men surrounding the little girl and I separated as the woman walked in our direction. She came right up to me and said, "This is our home base. It used to be a dilapidated house by the wayside, but we're fixing it up and making it ours. We're lucky that we found it when we did. We were fighting off a group of infected as we ran through the forest. We made it to this clearing and were able to separate the group. We killed them all, and then decided to become stationary here. The brick wall was already there when we arrived. Now, we're turning it into an impregnable base that can keep the infected away from us. What do you think?"

The base sure was impressive. The house was a large body sticking out in the middle of the clearing. Some men were moving supplies in and out of the house as I scanned it. With the brick wall surrounding it, it was definitely a safe place from the infected.

The woman spoke again, saying, "Construction is still going on and we have plenty of supplies. Come on inside. We'll get you a meal and some rest. We have to wait anyways for the other groups to return."

Other groups? What other groups? I thought about it in my mind.

There were probably more people that would call this place their home; the size of the house alone looked as if it could hold at least fifty people.

She sent the men with guns away, giving them orders to watch the perimeter until the others returned. She turned and waved us towards the entrance of the house.

We entered through two enormous wooden doors that led into a large expanse of space. From our vantage point, I could see a staircase leading up to a second story. To my right I saw a large dining room. It was covered in papers and maps. On the left was what looked like a large living room. There were boxes of supplies piled up over there.

The little girl wiggled out of my arms in excitement and began to walk around, gazing at the enormity of the place. The woman walked over to the nearest wall and turned on a board of switches. A low, dim light filled the rooms, making it somewhat easier to see.
The woman looked at me and said, "We have to have low-glow bulbs so we don't attract any outside or unwanted attention."

She motioned us towards the stairs so we could make our way onto the second story. I took another look around the room as we went up the stairs. The wood that comprised the house still seemed in good condition. The flower-patterned wallpaper was peeling from the walls, revealing the dark brown wood underneath. Cobwebs were in every corner of the house, no doubt crawling with spiders.

We came upon the second landing and looked around. Through the dim light filling the halls, I could see long corridors to my left and right. They seemed to stretch along endlessly through the house. The little girl led the way to the left as we followed her. She giggled as she skipped down the hall. She came to a stop at a door that had a large flower painted on it. We caught up to her and watched amusedly as she attempted to turn the rusted doorknob.

After a few moments, she stepped back and looked up at us in the dim light, expecting some sort of assistance. I walked up to the door and twisted the doorknob. It did not turn. I grasped it again tightly and put some extra muscle in it. The doorknob snapped off, but the door still opened up on its own in front of me. The ladies behind me let out small giggles when I looked back at them and shrugged my shoulders. They followed me as I stepped into the room and looked around.

It was a medium-sized room that was covered in flower wallpaper. The wallpaper was peeling from all sides. In the dim light of the hallway I could see a large bed on the right hand side. On the left was a large wooden dresser that looked ancient. There was a window on the far side of the room, which allowed me to see beyond the base and into the starry sky.

The little girl came in and jumped on the bed, causing it to shake along the floor. I placed the backpack on the floor and sat on the bed next to her. The woman stepped into the room and looked around. As she scanned the room, she said, "We still haven't explored all of this place."

She turned her gaze back to me and met my eyes. She paused, and then said, "I'm going to go back outside and wait for the others to return. You guys get some rest. We will have dinner when they get back. Until then, get some rest. You're going to need it."

I looked at the red haired woman peculiarly as she exited the room. The little girl stopped jumping and sat down next to me. She looked up at me and said quietly, "I want to eat now."

I retrieved the backpack and sat back down on the bed. I pulled out a package of the gummy bears and handed them to her.
She excitedly yelled, "Gummies!" and took the package from my hands.

She opened it quickly, but stopped as soon as it was open. She spent a few moments gazing at the package and contemplating something. Her smile faded, and her lips began to quiver. I watched as big tears began to roll down her face, hitting the bed covers and soaking in. We sat in silence for a few moments as I let her cry silently next to me.

I scooted over to her and put my arm around her shoulder. She leaned into me and began to sob. The gummies fell out of her hands and landed on the floor, spilling everywhere. I sat there silently, staring at the gummy bears spanning the floor.

I could faintly see the little smiles on the bears' faces. They were mocking the girl, reminding her of the death of her father. I held the little girl close as she continued to cry. She stopped after a while, and looked up at me with her tired eyes.

I couldn't find any words to say to comfort that little girl. I just stared into her wet eyes and gave a slow nod. The little girl nodded back and rose to her feet, squishing the bears on the floor. She wiped her eyes on her sleeve and gave me a weak smile. She told me, "It's okay. I'm going to be braver now."

I gave her a weak smile back, not knowing what to do. We stood for a moment in silence when we heard some thudding downstairs. The little girl looked at me and said, "More people are back! Let's go downstairs!"

At that, she ran out the door in the direction of the thuds. My heart ached for the little girl; she was so brave. I breathed out deeply, rose to my feet, and headed out the door.

TAPE #8

The little girl was waiting at the top of the stairs, looking at me expectantly. She gave me a smile and then turned her attention to the commotion downstairs. I stepped over next to her and looked down into the large space in the middle of the house.

It was packed with moving bodies; there had to be at least thirty people bustling about. Some of them were carrying guns, but for the most part the people below were without arms. They seemed like normal citizens I would have seen walking the sidewalks of the city.

I picked out the red haired woman in the midst of the crowd, remaining stationary amidst the flowing rivers of people. She looked up at us, motioning us to come in her direction. I grabbed the little girl's hand and led the way down. We came to the foot of the stairs, coming face to face with the raging rapids of the river. I clutched the girl's hand tightly and jumped in. We wiggled our way through the people and met the woman right in the middle of everything.

She greeted us with a smile and said, "It looks like everyone's here. We even found some survivors to bring back with us. We're in a hurry to set up everything for dinner. Are you guys hungry?" The little girl happily shouted, "Yup! I'm starving!" The red haired woman let out a loud laugh that caused a few heads to turn. She said, "Okay then. Follow me."

She led us through the current of people, taking us into the room that had been filled with supplies. When we stepped into the room, it was completely empty of the supplies I had seen before. The woman took a right hand turn in the room and led us through a door. On the other side of the door was a large kitchen of elegant taste. It was also extremely large. There were a few tables set up in the midst of the large space that were covered in different foods.

She walked up to the nearest table, picked up a peach, and tossed it over to me. I took a bite of the succulent, juicy peach. The juice ran down my chin, dripping onto the floor in front of me. I smiled with delight. I looked back over to the woman; she was handing the little girl a piece of bread. The little girl had a large smile on her face, grinning from ear to ear. She attempted to fit the whole piece of bread in her mouth, causing her cheeks to expand. I laughed aloud as I finished the peach in my hand. The woman grabbed herself a peach and began to eat it. As she ate, she said, "We're about to start serving dinner. We moved all of the supplies from the other room downstairs to the basement. Now we have enough room for everybody to eat.

You may be wondering why we have all of this food. A bunch of the groups that returned had brought food back from local areas. They looked for survivors as they scoured the area. Thankfully, they found enough food to last us a while. You guys make your way into the other room and we'll begin dinner shortly."

I nodded as I wiped the peach juice off my chin. The little girl walked over to me and we exited the room, leaving the red haired woman alone in the kitchen.

Dinner was a feast in and of itself. I don't really remember what we ate, but I definitely do recall the pleasurable pain my stomach felt as I sat in bed that night. We decided to make the room with the large flower on the door our room.

After saying goodnight to the others we had encountered and met during the meal, we went to our room. I put the little girl down to sleep next to me. I pulled the aged blankets up to her chin and sat down on the bed next to her. Before falling asleep, she pulled her little teddy bear out of her jacket and placed it on the bed next to her.

Then she pulled out the pack of gummy bears from within her jacket. She pulled them out slowly and looked at them with a sad expression. She placed the package on the floor and then turned her attention to the teddy bear. She pulled the raggedy bear close, smothering it with her love. She looked over at me, said goodnight, and fell asleep cradling her bear in her arms above the blanket.

I sat for a moment longer, staying awake and looking out into the sky outside. It was full of bright stars that spanned the entire space. I gazed at them, wondering how something so beautiful could exist in the midst of the chaos around me. I was looking out at the stars when I heard a light knock at the door.

I opened the door quietly and came face to face with the red haired woman. "Follow me" she said as she began to walk away down the hall. I nodded, looked back at the little girl to make sure she was asleep, and tip-toed outside, slowly closing the door behind me.

I met the woman at the base of the large set of stairs within the house. She nodded and led me into the dining room filled with papers and maps. There was a large table in the middle of the room. The table was surrounded with a group of ten people, four women including the red haired woman, and six men. She motioned me over to an empty chair and told me to sit.

As soon as I had taken a seat, a man across the table addressed me. He said, "You're probably wondering why we've called you here this evening. My daughter, the woman you met before with the red hair, has told me that you could be of some use to us. You were able to survive the infected from the city, making you a valuable asset to our team. You're here because we could use you to help us allocate supplies to keep our home base running and active.

I'm going to be frank with you, you have two options: you help us, or you leave. It's your choice. What do you say?"
I really didn't have much of a choice. Now that this man had gotten my attention, I gave him a long, hard look. He was a taller old man. His hair was snow white, save a few strands of black hair. He had white stubble all over his face. He wore a serious expression which made his rugged face seem fiercer. He was thin, but very muscular. He wore a faded red shirt with some sort of beer logo on it. I looked into his blue green eyes and could sense the finality of the decision I had to make. After taking a

second, I told him, "I'm here to help with whatever you need."

As soon as I had assured him of my assistance, his expression changed. He took on a warmer glow that put me a little more at ease. He said, "Good! Now let's get to business!"

He turned his attention away from me and began to address everyone at the large table. He spent a long time laying out the plans of operation in order to find supplies and keep the base running. He continuously pointed to the papers and maps, revealing his wisdom and knack for survival. The man pointed out that I would head up operations with his daughter, the red haired woman, in order to find and retrieve supplies. He spoke about the operations in the surrounding areas and beyond that I would help with.

After the meeting, the man told everyone to get some rest. I said goodnight to those who had attended the meeting; no names were given. The red haired woman escorted me back to my room. Before opening the door, she told me, "Don't mind him. He's really a nice guy. He just needed to make sure you would help us in order to stay here. Thank you for volunteering to help. I hope we can become friends and work well together." I replied, "Sure. Of course we can."

The woman gave me a grin and waved goodbye as she walked back down the hall. I entered the room quietly and sat down in the bed. I thought about my newfound responsibilities and the woman's father until sleep overtook me.

TAPE #9

The next day was when the operations the man had laid out began. The woman's father stationed a survivor to watch over the little girl as I went out. I went with the red haired woman to a nearby town and was able to gather supplies for the base. Luckily, we didn't run into any infected. We came back with some gas and food for everyone.

That night, after we had dinner and I put the little girl to bed, I went down to the dining room to debrief the woman's father on the operation that took place. I was commended for doing a great job by the red haired woman. Her father gave me an expectant look and said, "Good, because this is just the beginning."

Months passed like this: the endless hunt for supplies and resources in order to keep us going. I would return to our base every night to debrief the day and the operations that were performed. During that time, we were able to move around the immediate area closest to the base, gathering as much supplies as we could find. A lot of things happened during that period of what I would consider to be prosperity compared to where we are now.

A few new survivors were added to our makeshift family. We took them in gladly, realizing the implications they brought with them: we would need to ration our food with the addition of their presence, and we had to be more careful about letting just anyone in the base; it could mean trouble.

I say this because one man in that group was hiding a bite from an infected. We found out later that night how serious our overlook had been.

We placed the man in a room on the far right side of the house. Later that night, just before dinner, we heard thrashing from that area of the house. A few of us looked at each other in confusion, wondering if something was going wrong upstairs. Then an angry, shrill cry filled the house, sending chills down our spines and causing our hair to stand on end. We immediately knew what it was.

I looked around quickly, hoping the little girl and her companion were safe downstairs with us. They were huddled against the nearest wall; the little girl started to whimper as the woman clutched her close in her embrace.

I looked back over in the direction of some of the main personnel of the base; one man was sitting calmly, smoking a cigarette. The others were rushing upstairs, guns in hand. I stood up, but the man with the cigarette put his hand on my arm and pulled me back down. "Sit down and wait" he said. "They'll handle it." One last shrill cry filled the house, and then the sounds of a round of gunshots went off. Then everything was silent.

I stood up and stepped into the main space of the house. Two men were dragging the deformed being down the stairs and out the door. A large trail of thick blood was left behind them. The red haired woman stood at the top of the stairs, blood soaked onto her face. Her father was standing next to her, covered in blood as well. He stepped down the stairs alone and called everyone to attention. He yelled at us, saying, "That's it! We can't take anyone else on in this place! No one else is allowed to come here! If you see any survivors, you give them some food and water and send them packing! Not only do we need to begin to ration our food because of these new people, but we also have to clean up this mess at the same time! No dinner for anyone tonight! Go to bed!"

With that address, we all made our way upstairs. The little girl held my hand tightly as we walked up the stairs while staring at the blood trail. It was difficult to sleep that night, fearing that another infected might attack. The little girl and I didn't fall asleep until the dawn had come to greet us with its warm light.

The little girl became good friends with the survivor put in charge over her. She was an elderly woman that had been saved in a nearby town. She had hid in her car for three days, starving herself and drawing no attention as the infected ran about. A group of those at the base had performed an operation to get food when they came across her. She was saved and brought back to the base to recover. Since she was sixty-four years old, she wasn't allowed to go out on any operations. So, the red haired woman's father put her in charge of my little girl.

They became instant friends. Every time I would return from operations, I would immediately make my way up the stairs of the house and go into my room; it was their "home base."

One thing I truly appreciated about the woman is that she encouraged the little girl to draw. She encouraged her to draw everything from her favorite foods and animals to her feelings about that day.

Drawings began to fill the room, spanning the walls and covering up the peeling wallpaper in the room. Where they found crayons and paper, I'll never know. Nevertheless, it made me happy to see the little girl preoccupying her time and developing a friendship with someone. They bonded over those months, forming a bond only good sisters can have.

The red haired woman and I bonded during that time as well. We went on missions to scavenge for supplies on our own as a pair. We would have long talks about our lives and everything that was going on as we trudged through the forest to find our location. The woman became acquainted with my story as I became knowledgeable of hers.

One day, I told her of my experience in the hospital and the loss of my wife and unknown child. As soon as I had told her, she stopped immediately on the forest floor and became silent for a few moments. A tear ran down her face as she uttered, "I'm so sorry. I had no idea."

I lied and told her it was fine, and that now it was just a painful memory. I also told her about what had occurred on the military base before finding ourselves with her and her father's company. She was shocked at everything that had happened. She said that she felt horrible for the little girl, to see her lose her father in such a horrific way. She seemed too sincere in her reaction to my story, and a few days later I understood why.

That was when she told me her story. We were returning from an unsuccessful mission to a nearby town to see if we could find some goods. We stopped on the forest floor underneath the shade of a large pine tree. She looked me in the eyes and just spilled her guts; just like that.

I listened carefully as she relayed her journey to me. She was a military brat, always moving when she was a kid. Her father was a sniper, and her mother was an army nurse. Her parents met after her father had returned from a mission. He had been shot in the right shoulder, and her mother was the nurse who tended to him. They got to know each other and became good friends.

Then her father left for two years in order to work on a base in Europe. They kept in touch that entire time, allowing their love to build up. As soon as he had returned from his leave, they met up again. They dated and ended up getting married a year later.

The red haired woman told me that all she had ever known was boxes. Every few years, she could expect to go home one evening to a house packed with taped boxes. She would begin to cry as her parents went up to her, sweeping her up into their arms and trying to console her. Their excuse was always that it was time for a new adventure. She believed that lie all of her life.

She grew up like every other kid, save the constant movement from one state to the next. She went through high school and went to college in order to study as a nurse. She told me she had always admired her mother for saving lives every day. The long nights that she was away from her were worth it because she knew her mother would be out saving the world, one soldier at a time. She had just begun graduate school when the outbreak began.

As soon as it happened, her father had gone to get her and bring her back home. She expected to see her mother again, as happy as she ever was. Instead, she went back to a scene that would change her life forever.

Her father had been silent the whole way back home. That wasn't like him at all; he was usually very talkative and would never shut up. Whenever she would try to start up a conversation, her father would zone off in the middle of his sentence and become preoccupied with something else. When she had gotten home, she understood.

She told me that the first thing she heard was the racking cough that spurted from the lungs of her mother. She had just placed her bags on the floor when her father grabbed her by the arm and pulled her into the living room. As soon as she had taken a seat on the sofa, her father spilled the truth.

Her mother had been very sick lately. Ever since she had left the army hospital two days prior, she had been falling to pieces. Her hair was falling out; her skin was beginning to become pale and seemed to tear at the seams. Her normally carefree demeanor had turned into one of aggression. Thick, green mucus spurted from her mouth with every cough.

As soon as she had heard the truth, she ran into the room to see her mother. It was worse than she ever could have imagined and the words that her father shared did not due her horrible condition justice.

Over the next few hours, the normally strong and willful woman she had known disintegrated right in front of her. During those hours, her mother lost the ability to speak. She was only able to make grunts and squeals of pain as the red haired woman did her best to retain composure despite the tears flowing down her face. She sat with her mother until the end, when the last gasp of life left her lungs.

That was where she stopped. We stood there in the shade of a tree, completely silent. The red haired woman spent a few moments looking down at her shoes, waiting for me to respond. I stood there silently, not knowing what to do.

After a few more moments of awkward silence, I walked over to her and placed my hand on her shoulder. Immediately, she leaned into my chest and began to sob uncontrollably. I let her cry into my chest and held her, feeling the utter devastation in her heart.

We stood there for quite a while until she was able to stop. She wiped her eyes and thanked me for listening to her; she had never told anyone that story before. I gave her a weak smile, took her hand in mine, and we made our way back to the base.

The red haired woman's father called a meeting that night, relaying plans for another operation. We were beginning to run low on supplies, and we needed to find some in order to keep the base running. During the meeting, he brought out a map I had never seen before. He pulled it out of his jacket pocket and unfolded it. As soon as he had placed it in the center of everyone, he said, "I don't want to have to go here, but I know we need to do it."

He scanned the room, looking into the curious eyes of everyone present. He pointed at the center of the map and continued on, "There's a town called Tuckerton farther out than the usual operations we have performed around here. It's a larger town, almost a city. It is way different than all of the places we've been going to. We need to go there; they have everything we need.

However, it's crawling with infected. I'm not going to lie to you; we're desperate for supplies. We're beginning to run low on everything. We have two options: we go to Tuckerton, or we kick some people to the curb.

I'll just say it now. Tuckerton is going to be a large scale operation that requires at least twenty of the thirty eight of us. Yes, it will be dangerous; it's almost a suicide mission. But we need to find some way of still surviving here.

Now, I've presented the options, and I'll leave the decision up to the rest of you. Let's vote."

The vote was split down the middle. The vote came down to one man; me. They waited anxiously for my response. I became nervous as I began to realize the weight of the decision I had to make. My palms began to sweat. The expectant look on everyone's faces to choose their side made my heart beat fast. I finally spoke up and confidently said, "I think we should try to find supplies there in Tuckerton."

I was received with some smiles of approval as well as sneers of disgust. That meeting settled it; we were going to Tuckerton. That would be the biggest mistake of our lives.

TAPE #10

Tuckerton.

That was where everything went to hell. I think back on all that happened in that town, and hate rises up within me. Hate for mistakes, hate for failures, and hate above all for the infected.

We rose early in the morning for the mission. There was a group of twenty-two of us going. We were to meet at the crack of dawn, ready to go. I woke up to a dark sky filled with stars. I snuck out of bed, got dressed, and headed out of my room. The little girl lay sound asleep in the bed, clutching her ragged bear.

I made my way downstairs and outside. In the midst of the darkened base, I could see the red haired woman waiting at the front gate. I made my way over to her so we could wait for the others to join us. She gave me a warm smile as I came up to meet her. We stood around chatting as the sun came up.

We turned our attention to a group of men and women exiting the house in a large cluster, making their way towards us. The woman's father was at the front of the group; he had a look of determination that gave him a commanding presence as he stepped up to us.

He walked right past us, going to the large metal doors of the wall surrounding the base. He stopped and turned around, facing the entire group. He addressed us with a good morning and got right down to business.

He said, "Okay everyone! Listen up! Today is going to be the biggest mission we've carried out so far. It's going to be dangerous. You need to listen to everything I tell you.

We are going to split into three teams: team one will be in charge of gathering food supplies from the convenient store. Team two will be responsible for getting fuel from the cars in the area. Finally, team three will have to look in houses in the surrounding area for anything useful. I'm going to split you into your teams and then we'll move out, heading to Tuckerton from different positions. That way we can't all be attacked at the same time. Does everyone understand? Good. Let's get started."

He proceeded to divide the group into three teams. He placed himself as the head of the team to gather fuel. The red haired woman was head of the group going to the convenient store. I was chosen to be a member of the team that would check out the surrounding area.

The leader of my group was a man that looked to be about my age. He had dirty blond hair and wild blue eyes. He was of average height and carried himself with an air of self-reliance. He had blond stubble all over his face. Since I had known him, he always carried a cigarette tucked behind his right ear and another burning away in his yellow mouth. He was tough; I had seen him slay his fair share of infected and beyond. The woman's father would spend time with him some nights sitting outside, smoking under the starry sky.

He was a warrior; at least that's what everyone called him. He always carried a fire axe with him, using it to slay countless infected. He treated it almost like a child, taking much time to make sure it was sharpened and clean for every mission. I couldn't have asked for a better leader.

After getting our team placement, we all set out for Tuckerton. The father's team was to enter Tuckerton from the North, the woman's team was to enter from the East, and the team I was in was to enter from the West. The teams parted, leaving the grounds of the base and heading into different parts of the dense forest all around.

Once we had gone into the woods for a while, the warrior pointed to a fork with two trees, signaling us to stop. Once we had stopped, he motioned us to gather around him as he pulled a piece of paper from his jacket. It was the same map the red haired woman's father had shown everyone the night before.

There was a wide red arrow that led from our base to the city of Tuckerton. It stopped in the midst of a large series of houses surrounding the main center of town.

The warrior said, "This is where we're headed. We have the most dangerous part of the mission; we can't really know what to expect. We have to be on our toes the entire time. Make sure all of you stick close to me. When we get there, I will be splitting us up so we can cover more ground and gather more supplies. Until then, we have to make it through the back end of Tuckerton to reach our destination. Be careful to conserve your ammo and rely on your close combat weapons more so as not to make much noise. You never know what could be lurking in the forest. Let's move out."

As I stood up, I placed my hand on the small of my back, feeling for the black pistol the red haired woman had given me months prior. It had a full clip, and I had one other clip tucked away in the pocket of my pants. I looked into my dominant right hand, admiring how the blade of my machete shone in the light of the forest.

I quickly recalled the various operations during the past few months. The machete had been a close companion, helping me escape some hairy situations. I saw my reflection in the blade; I looked tired and worn out. It was as if I had gained a lifetime since the outbreak began so long ago. I smiled at myself, musing at the idea that I was officially an old man in my own eyes. I looked up to see the rest of my group moving on, trailing behind the warrior. I followed them past the fork and deeper into the forest.

We had the farthest distance to go to end up at the back end of Tuckerton. The forest was silent as we trudged our way through. There wasn't any noise around us besides the crunching of the leaves under out feet and the sound of running water whenever we would pass by the occasional stream. I could see the sun peeking through the dense trees that made a roof over our heads. I don't know how long we made our way through the dense forest, but it felt like an eternity.

After a seemingly endless length of time, we came to a small clearing with a large hill protruding out of the middle of the ground. The warrior motioned us to the peak of it. Once everyone had made it to the summit, he motioned us to stop and take a rest. We placed all of our gear on the ground in front of us and sat on the grass.

After a few moments of rest, the warrior motioned us over to him. We surrounded him as he pointed out that Tuckerton was not far off from here. I followed the line his finger made from where we were to where Tuckerton lied on the horizon. I could make out a faint skyline formed by the buildings of our destination. Columns of smoke were rising into the sky, creating an evil cloud over the town. It was a warning; I know that all too well now.

After a few more moments of rest, we picked up our gear and headed down the opposite side of the hill. We made our way through much more of the dense forest, but this time it was different. There was still the same stale silence stagnating in the air, but as we neared our destination, a horrible smell filled the space around us. It was a familiar smell, but the stench of it was overpowering.

It was the smell of death and decay filling the air. We continued to trudge our way through despite the overpowering odor. After entering through an area of thick brush, we came upon a brick wall. The warrior squatted near to the ground and motioned us silently over. We quietly crept over to him.

He whispered to us, saying, "Here we are. This is the edge of Tuckerton. We don't know what to expect beyond this wall. The devastation here is likely to be catastrophic. Remember not to panic. Is everyone ready? Let's go."

None of us were prepared for what lay behind that wall. The warrior leaped over without hesitating. He made a whistling sound that let us know the coast was clear and that we could head over. Everyone motioned me to go over first. I shrugged my shoulders and clamored over the wall. I landed on my feet next to the warrior. The devastation of Tuckerton was worse than I could have ever imagined.

I found myself in a large neighborhood that was completely torn to shreds. The houses and streets were splattered with red and were falling apart. Smoke was making its way into the sky from multiple fires.

Bodies filled the streets. There were a few cars lining the streets that seemed to be long out of commission. In the distance I could see more pillars of smoke reaching up into the air, desperately choking out the blue sky that was no longer overhead. It had been blanketed by the black hopelessness of the devastation of Tuckerton long ago. Everything was in a state of horror and chaos; I didn't want to be there.

I stepped forward and began to walk up the street as the warrior waited for the others to make their way over the wall. I took another long look at my surroundings; a pit began to form in my stomach, causing me to feel nauseous. A cold sweat began to form on my forehead and my hands as I scanned the bodies piled in the streets.

There were two kinds of bodies there: the bodies of dead infected, and the bodies of their victims. I stopped halfway up the block as the warrior called out to me to wait for everyone else. As I stood there waiting, one body caught my attention.

It was the body of an infected. It appeared to have once been a young boy. I tried to imagine it as a young boy innocently playing in the streets with his friends. He looked to be the same age as my little girl back at the base.

He would have been happy to play soccer in the streets, ignoring the girls watching because they would be full of coodies. He would have gone to school and been a good boy, making sure he did all he could to make his parents happy. He would have had a bright future, maybe as a doctor or teacher or something of that sort; someone that could make a difference in the world at least.

But that future had been lost a long time ago due to the infection. This boy was no longer human; he was some sort of demon. He was lying face up on the ground. His pale eyes seemed to search the sky overhead, looking for some sort of break in the black covering above. The twisted body of the monster seemed to bend in many different directions all at once. Half of its hair had fallen out; the hair that remained had turned a whitish color, making the dried green slime plastered on its face that much more noticeable.

What struck me the most about this small infected were its hands. Its left hand was lying palm up on the ground. It seemed to be expecting something to be placed there. It made me wonder if that monster had any hopes beyond its primal hunger for flesh. Maybe it was waiting to grasp onto something it never got the chance to receive. Maybe it was still partially human, grasping onto its fleeting existence as the infection took hold. Then I saw the other hand.

Its right hand was clutching at its heart. It was clutching its chest so tightly that wells of its polluted blood were forming at the fingers. It seemed as though it was trying to dig its heart out of its chest.

Could that monster have wanted to die, knowing its only purpose was to feed and kill the ones it had once loved and nothing more? As the transformation took place, had this once young boy wanted the sweet release of death in order to avoid hurting those around him? I stood still, gazing into the seemingly sorrowful eyes of the monster. I hardly noticed the warrior who had come and stood next to me.

"Pretty rough, huh?" he said to me after a few moments of silence. I didn't respond as I could not stop staring at those hands. He grabbed me by the shoulder and waited for me to face him. When I did, he spit the cigarette he was smoking out of his mouth and said, "I know. Trust me, I know. We're not so different. I can see it in your eyes. I can't help but think it when it hits me all of a sudden. Is there anything left of that boy in there? Had he wanted to die? How could such an evil exist that can ravage the innocent body of a child? Do you want to know the answer?"

I looked deeply into his wild blue eyes and nodded. He looked down at the body and stated, "I don't know. That's the answer. I just don't know. Something inside me tells me that I might never know. I hate that. I hate not knowing. I hate being stuck in this place. I hate that I can't live a normal life ever again. I hate that every second of my life is fleeting because I have nothing to live for. I hate it. I want to be like that boy. I want to be dead."

He looked back into my eyes. I could see tears beginning to form in his. He continued on: "But I know I can't do that. I can't be weak; I can't let the evil in this world win. I want to die so badly I can taste it, but I just know I can't let the evil here take any more of what is left around me. That is why I can't stop killing the infected and surviving. Not for anyone or anything; not even for myself. Simply because I just can't let the evil win. You understand me. I can always see it in your eyes. You want death to swallow you whole and never spit you back out. You have nothing left. You want it to be over. But I'm telling you, we have to fight. That's all there is to it. Nothing more, nothing less."

We stood there in silence as the others looked on. After another minute, he wiped his tears on his sleeve, shouldered his axe, and said, "Let's go, we need to survive. For you especially, you need to for that little girl back at base. You need to live for her no matter how badly you want to give up. You're all she's got."

He stepped away from me and made his way back to the main group. The little girl flashed into my mind. The warrior was right. I was being selfish by wanting to give up and end it all. She needed me. She was my little girl. I was all that she had. I promised I would never leave her, no matter what. Everyone else had failed to fulfill their promises to her; I wouldn't be another.

I took one last look at those hands, turned my attention back to the group, and made my way back over to them. As soon as I had stepped into the cluster, the warrior began.

"We're here. This is just a small taste of the devastation going on here. Be careful; this place will be flooded with infected. Be quick and silent. Use your melee weapons only, saving the guns for emergency situations. We are going to split into three teams in order to gather supplies. We will be focusing on ten major neighborhoods in this area. The sun is high in the sky now. We have until sunset to be back here at the brick wall. Once sunset hits, we're leaving. I won't risk being here when this place gets filled with those monsters. Everyone get it? All right, let's do this and get the hell out of here."

He proceeded to break our group up into three separate teams. He kept me in his group. He sent the first and second groups out and then began to lead our group down a series of streets until we came to a neighborhood that was in worse condition than where we had begun. We made our way halfway down the block and stopped.

In the midst of the stale silence, the warrior spoke in a whisper. He told us to split in half, making two teams that could scour the area and find whatever was useful. He split up the group and kept me at his side. Our team was going to go on the far end of the street and search while the other team remained closer to the beginning of the block.

We separated and made our way to our destinations. We stopped at the end of the street, in front of a blue two story house with a large tree in front of it. The house was in a state of decay as the paint was flaky, the windows broken, and broken glass was lining the main pathway leading up to the front door. The tree was still barely alive as a few leaves clung to its branches. There was a long streak of red across its large trunk that connected to a blood trail leading down the street.

The warrior went up to the main door of the house and tried to open it; it was unlocked. He motioned us over and carefully stepped inside. I took a deep breath and entered into the darkened house.

Once inside the house, I could see somewhat. The light from the sun emanated through the broken windows and provided a vibrant light that filled the main doorway. There were three places to go: to the right was the dining room and kitchen area, to the left was a living room and a door leading to the basement downstairs, and directly in front of us was a staircase leading to a second floor.

We split into three groups of two and headed to different areas of the house. The warrior and I took the staircase to the second floor. We reached the second landing and scanned the area. There was a short hallway with three rooms: one on the left, one on the right, and a third room that appeared to be a bathroom. A large pool of dried blood was in the center of the hallway. Bloody smears lined the walls, supporting the idea of a struggle that had taken place long ago. The door to the bathroom was wide open, revealing no danger there.

The warrior signaled me to take the door on the left as he began to open the door to the right. I slowly turned the doorknob with my left hand, my machete ready to slice through anything in my path. I opened the door and peeked inside.

I looked at the floor in the sunlight shining through a nearby broken window to see two people, a man and a woman, lying on the ground. The man was lying on top of the face down woman with his hands covering her as if to shield her. The woman had been eaten away at the neck, almost severing her head from her body. The man had been eaten almost entirely halfway through. I could see his spine and internal organs in the dried, thick blood. A large pool had formed and dried, spanning most of the room.

I swallowed hard and began to search the room. I ransacked a nearby dresser, a closet, and a small bathroom connected to the room. As I finished putting everything I had found in my pack, I heard the muffled sound of footsteps coming from the room across from me. I turned my head as the screams filled the air. The first thing I heard was the warrior yell out, "Dammit!"

I saw a small figure on his back, trying to get its jaws around his neck. He was holding its head a few inches from his neck as he called out my name. He had dropped his axe a few feet away from him, and the infected child attacking him would not let up. I held my machete tight as I dropped my pack and ran towards him. I bolted across the hallway and into the room. I raised my machete above my head and got ready to deliver a powerful blow to the creature. As I prepared to swing, a strong force threw me from my feet to a nearby wall. My vision went blurry for a moment as the blood began to swell within my head.

As my vision cleared, I saw another infected standing where I once stood. This one was much larger, and looked to have once been a teenage boy. It was tall and muscular; perhaps it had once been a football player. My eyes began to search the ground for my machete; it was lying in between its legs, shining in the light of the room. It turned its attention towards the warrior and began to claw at his back. A painful cry filled the air as it tore through his shirt and into his flesh.

I snapped into action, got to my feet, and ran to my machete. I picked it up in one fell swoop and put its shining blade into the right shoulder of the infected. A howl filled the air as I pulled the blade out and stabbed it into the small of its back.

The infected child was still clinging to the warrior, edging its way towards his neck. The warrior was fighting as best he could, but fighting two infected at once was draining all he had. As I pulled the machete out of the back of the larger infected, it turned towards me and threw me into the hallway. I landed on my back in the midst of the dried blood pool. It leaped in my direction, intending to land on top of me.

As it flew through the air, I tucked my knees into my chest and prepared for its landing. It landed on top of me, and I used my legs to propel it away from me and down the stairway. It banged against the wall and tumbled down the stairs.

I sat up to the sight of the warrior throwing himself against the doorway, knocking the small infected from him onto the floor beside me. My eyes got wide as it scrambled to its feet beside me and let its white, hateful eyes focus on me. Stunned by its evil gaze, I attempted to raise my machete for an attack. The monster grabbed ahold of the blade, pulled it from my hand, and threw it down the stairway. The creature let green spittle drip from its small mouth as it seemed to smile at me.

It jumped on top of me and tried to edge its head close to my neck for a bite. As it edged its face closer to mine, the blade of the fire axe landed directly into the head of the attacking infected. Blood and cranial fluid exploded out of its head and landed all over my face. I closed my eyes and felt the warm liquid flow down my face. I heard a thump as its body landed next to me on the floor. I used my sleeve to wipe my face and opened my eyes.

The warrior was standing above me, fire axe in hand. He had a look of satisfaction on his face as he gazed at the body of the dead infected. I took a deep breath, thanked him, and got up. He told me, "Don't thank me yet. The other one is downstairs waiting for us."

As he said this, his wild eyes began to flare up with pleasure. He wanted to find the other infected and exact his revenge upon it. He gave me a twisted smile as he turned from me and headed towards the stairs. I saw his torn back as he walked away. There were three large rips in his back, and blood was seeping out of all of them. His shirt was beginning to turn a darker shade of blue as the blood was soaking into the fabric. I stood there for a second, gave a small kick to the dead infected, and followed behind.

We walked down the stairs and stopped at their base. The house was strangely quiet. The warrior focused on the silence, waiting for a noise to reveal the creature's location.

I whispered, "What about the others searching the house? Should we warn them?" He told me, "No. We need to find it quietly. It could be waiting to ambush us. The others can take care of themselves if it goes their way."

The warrior signaled for me to go in the direction of the team that went to check out the basement as he made his way in the direction of the dining room and kitchen. I walked through the living room and stopped in front of the closed door leading to the basement below.

A pit began to form in my stomach as I reached for the handle. I did my best to ignore it as I opened the door to the darkness below. I took a few steps down, searching for a light to turn on.

My hand found a switch and flipped it on. The light that slowly flickered on illuminated the basement. A wide array of boxes and merchandise formed walls and columns in the large space. Various appliances, books, trophies, games, clothes, and other memorabilia served as bricks in the construction of this large makeshift maze. It created an eerie feeling in my gut. It was inviting me in, beckoning me to explore it, get lost in it, and never find my way back out.

I came to the bottom of the stairs and stopped at the entrance of the maze. I whispered the names of my teammates to get a reply; there was no answer. I looked over my shoulders, took a deep breath, and entered the basement's maze.

It was much larger than I thought. I was able to turn a few corners crammed with stuff. After another turn, I found a straight way that extended for a good length of space. I made it halfway when a side of the maze came crashing down right in front of me. It sounded like an avalanche as many things fell, blocking the path before me. I stood there for a second, thinking about how lucky it was that I had not ended up at the bottom of that crash. I scanned the debris, looking for anything useful since I could not go any further.

In the silence, I began to hear the sound of something coughing. It seemed to be coming from the pile in front of me. I moved a few things, and could see the arm of a human being. It was the long, slender arm of one of my teammates. I immediately grabbed it and pulled it with all of my might. My teammate came sliding out of the debris, pulling a few books and shirts with him. I dragged him a few feet away from the pile and sat him up against a nearby dresser. He looked up at me and I immediately knew.

He began to speak, but I didn't hear him at first. All I could focus on was the small bite that was on his left thigh. It was leaking blood into his pants and out onto the floor. I looked into his eyes and could see that his pupils had grown significantly smaller. He was on the verge of becoming an infected, and it was too late to try to get him any help.

His voice began to reach my ears as he talked about what had happened. An infected had been in the basement, waiting for them to go down. His partner had been attacked from behind as it threw him to the ground and took a large bite out of his neck, instantly killing him. Then the monster made its way after the man here. He ran a few turns, but the creature caught up to him and managed to take a bite out of his leg as he ran. He had turned and killed the infected with a metal bar he was carrying. He had begun to make his way out of the maze when he started to feel weak and sick. He walked until he toppled over, landing in the pile of debris in front of me.

He looked up at me and said, "I can see the look in your eyes. Please don't kill me. I know it's too late, but please don't kill me. Just leave me here, go upstairs, lock the door, and forget about me. I just don't want to die."

His eyes were filling with tears as he said this. I looked at him, his bleeding bite, and then at the machete in my right hand. I did want to spare him, but I knew it was too much of a risk to let a monster run loose. What if it escaped and killed someone? It would be my fault. What if, since it knew where the base was, it got a group of infected and made a large scale attack on the base?

My little girl and the other survivors flashed into my mind. I could see them being eaten alive by him and his infected friends. I could see him chewing on my little girl's neck, spilling blood all over the floor of our room, smiling as he did so. I began to slowly bring my machete in front of me, knowing what I had to do. He saw this; he knew my intention.

He quickly grabbed my machete and held onto its blade. Thick red blood was flowing down his arm as he held the blade fast. "No! Don't" he cried aloud. I could see fear in his eyes; a fear of death.

In his panic he began to reach for his belt and pull a revolver from his side. The same scene of him killing those I loved flashed into my mind once more. I instinctively pulled the black pistol from the small of my back and put two bullets right into his forehead. Blood splattered against the dresser as the life left his body. His hand released the blade and fell to the floor. I quickly picked up his revolver, tucked it into my belt, and began to make my way back out of the maze.

I dared not look back, for fear I would regret what I had done. I found myself running, trying to escape the guilt that was beginning to rise up in my throat. I had killed an innocent man.

I tried to justify it by saying that he was about to become a monster. But he wasn't a monster yet; he had still been a man when I killed him. I reminded myself of my little girl, saying in my mind that I had to do it to protect her and everyone else on that base. That seemed to quell my heart as I tried to suppress the murder I had just committed.

I came to the entrance of the basement and walked out into the living room. The warrior was on a nearby couch, lying on his stomach. The two remaining teammates of our group were placing bandages on his back and curing his wound. He tried to sit up as he waited for me to tell him where the others were. I looked at him and shook my head. I pulled out the revolver and let the sunlight reflect off of its metallic surface. The warrior nodded and lied back down. I went over and sat down next to him as he was being treated.

I dared not look at anyone; I was afraid they would see the guilt in my eyes. I listened to the silence of the house, taking it all in. I let myself become numb as I drifted off into my thoughts about all that had happened. After some time, I found myself looking at the warrior standing in front of me.

I snapped out of my trance and stood up. "Let's move out", he said with finality. I nodded in agreement and followed the three last members of my group out the door. We came back outside onto the street and scanned the neighborhood.

The warrior turned to face us and stated, "We still need to finish the mission. Here's what we're going to do: we remain as a pack, scouring the rest of this neighborhood for supplies. Let's get this done quickly and quietly, and then meet up with the other groups we sent out. We don't have much time left; the sun is getting closer to the horizon. All right, let's move out."

We started on the left side of the neighborhood, moving quickly from house to house. The warrior avoided any lower levels and higher levels of the houses we explored. Our main focus became scavenging for food and some tools as we cleared kitchens of non-perishables and knives.

When I asked why we were collecting all of these kitchen knives, one of the members of our group responded, "You never know when you'll need a knife." That answer confused me more than it answered my question, but I just shrugged my shoulders and let it go. We didn't experience any more encounters with any infected until we scavenged on the right side of the neighborhood.

We made our way through, and at the sixth house down one of our members was taken by surprise by a large infected that was hiding in a laundry room. He was bitten by the infected before we could kill it, and the warrior had no qualms with putting the fire axe right in the middle of his chest. After stopping him, the warrior beheaded him to make sure he would stay dead. Then it became the three of us: the warrior, myself, and a sturdy woman who could definitely handle herself.

We continued on with our mission, finishing the block and slaying the few infected that crossed our path. After we had ransacked the final kitchen, we made our way outside and stopped in the middle of the street. The sun was beginning to lower in the sky, revealing that we were quickly running out of time.

The warrior had us take our packs off and see what we had gathered. We had a plethora of goods; a large amount of what we had were non-perishables and the rest of our plunder comprised of knives and other tools. The warrior gave us a weak smile and stated, "I think we've done a good job. Let's go and try to find another group nearby since we have enough time left to spare."

The light of the sun was revealing how the warrior was suffering

73

from his wounds. He began to wince in pain as he tried to lift his pack onto his shoulders. His skin had begun to turn pale, revealing the loss of blood he had suffered from the attack earlier.

Once we had gotten our packs on, we began to walk down the block to the main street. When we stopped there, I turned to the warrior and asked him, "Are you okay? I can carry your pack for you." He snapped back at me as his wild eyes flared up in anger. "I'm fine! Worry about yourself, okay?"

I looked down at my feet and turned my attention towards the next block. I started walking ahead of him in that direction. After a few steps, I turned around to see the woman right behind me, her attention forward as well. I looked past her to see the warrior standing where we had left him. We stopped and waited for him to come join us.

After a few minutes, he walked in our direction. He came straight up to me, bypassing the woman with us, and put his hand on my shoulder. "I'm sorry" he said as he looked me right in the face. "I guess I've just lost a lot of blood."

I nodded in understanding, seeing that he was just trying to hold on to whatever he had left. He turned his attention towards the woman and said, "Let's go."

He led the way down the main street with the two of us following closely behind. We walked for three or four blocks as the sun hung high overhead. As we neared a corner, the warrior instinctively turned around, grabbed both of us by straps on our packs, and threw us into some bushes lining the sidewalk. We landed in a backyard filled with lush green grass. The warrior placed his hands over our mouths and whispered, "There's a bunch of infected gathering over there. It looks like there are a ton of them. Keep quiet. We're going to see what's going on."

We stood up and crept to the edge of the house nearby. We walked along its side and peeked around the corner, focusing on the commotion down the street.

There was a crowd of at least twenty infected gathering in the middle of the street. They were tearing away at something as blood and articles of clothing were flying in the air around them. I thought how unfortunate the victim of their hunger was as they tore it apart, piece by piece. We watched on for a while as they continued to ravage the corpse of whatever the thing was.

A few of the infected there had their fill and swiftly moved away as blood continued to flow down their demonic faces. As more of them began to clear, I realized that there was more than one body they had been feeding on. I could see nine or ten corpses lying in the middle of the street, each near to each other. A few more infected left, allowing me to see even clearer.

My blood ran cold when I saw the whole picture: the corpses in the middle of the street were one of the groups that the warrior had sent out and two infected that had been slain alongside them. My hand gripped the handle of my machete so tight that the muscles in my hand began to hurt. Anger was swelling up inside of me as I stared at the corpses lying in there. Before I realized it, I had stepped out from the safety of the shadows of the house we were hiding by and ended up on the sidewalk in front of it.

I heard a scream from behind me as I realized what I had done. The woman was yelling for me to come back, making the trouble I had gotten myself in much, much worse. I snapped out of my anger and looked around the street. I was able to meet the glance of at least fourteen infected that had turned their attention towards me.

A cold sweat broke out all over my body as I took a slow step backwards. The infected watching me stood still for a second, then their shrill cries of evil began to fill the air. "Run! We gotta get outta here!" the warrior shouted at me.

I immediately turned around, breaking into a sprint to the side of the house. The warrior and the woman began to run to the back of the house as I followed. As soon as I passed the side of the house, the shrill cries of the infected were ringing loudly in my ears, seeming to come from all directions. We ran through a few backyards, throwing ourselves over walls and through foliage. We made it onto a main street and were spotted by more infected. We were cut off in both directions, and had to retreat down the street we were on. The warrior called out, "There! That large house at the end of the street!"

We made a full on sprint through the decaying corpses and dilapidated cars and ran right into a large red house. I led the charge into the house and slammed the door shut as soon as the last of us entered. I bolted the door shut and turned around to face the warrior and the woman.

I felt immense pain as the warrior's fist hit me square in the face, knocking me to the ground. He began to kick me in the chest and stomach as he yelled, "You stupid idiot! Why did you do that!? You're going to get all of us killed!"

The woman tried to stop him from beating me, which was a huge mistake. As I lie on the ground holding my stomach and tasting the blood running down my face, the warrior turned, slapped the woman, and threw her over a table and into a wall. He went over to her, bent down, and began to slap her hard. His smacks resounded in the air as he yelled at her too. "And you! What the hell were you thinking yelling out like that! You're just as stupid as he is! I ought to shoot you and him right in the face!"

I managed to stand up. I tried to walk over to the warrior. He stood up, turned around to face me, and let his wild blue eyes flare up. He came right at me, tackling me to the floor. He got up, dragged me around a corner to the kitchen, picked me up, and slammed me on a counter by a sink. He began to run water, filling the sink.

After it was mostly filled, he turned me over onto my stomach as I tried to fight him off. I lost the fight as he turned me completely over and began to dunk my head under the water. I swallowed a lungful of water and began to panic as he held me down. I could feel that he had climbed on top of me, placing all of his weight on my back. He continued to yell at me while continuously dunking me, allowing me to come up for air every few seconds. After a few more dunks and a few more large swallows of water, he threw me off the counter and onto the floor.

I lied on the ground, coughing and sputtering as I tried to breathe. The warrior slid down the counter, sitting on the floor. I looked over to see the woman walking over to us, holding her right shoulder. She came over and sat on the floor. I began to cough weakly as I sat up as well.

We sat in silence for a few moments, only hearing the sounds of the infected banging and scratching at the door. The warrior stood up and said, "Pick yourselves up. We have to get moving."

We slowly stood up and picked up the gear we had dropped. We followed the warrior onto the second story of the house we were in and stopped in its main hallway. We stood still as the warrior began to open doors and look around the house. He opened the door to a large bathroom, went inside, and came back out a few seconds later. "I think I found a way out", he said with a grim look on his face. The woman and I nodded in quick agreement, careful not to anger him any further.

He continued on, "The problem is we've caught the attention of too many infected. There's some right below the window. The only way out of here is to climb out, make our way through this large backyard, and hop over that wall. But there's too many of them gathered out there. There's already too many of them outside in front as well. We have to think of a distraction."

"How about a lot of noise?" I said shyly, hoping to be received well. "Or fire" said the woman, having the same sheepish demeanor as I did. "Not bad" said the warrior as he thought to himself. After a few seconds, he looked up at us and said, "Why not do both?" The woman and I looked at each other and nodded. The warrior spoke, "Now that we have a plan, let's get started."

He sent the woman and I down to the first level of the house to look for anything flammable and metallic so we could fashion something to make noise. As soon as we reached the landing of the first floor, the reality of the situation grabbed us. The banging of the infected seemed to edge through the walls, surrounding us and closing us in. We could hear their cries of hunger coming through the walls and into our bones.

We began to quicken our pace now, gathering all of the supplies we could to create this distraction that would allow us to escape. After gathering some of the resources in the house, we went back upstairs where the warrior was waiting for us with some supplies of his own. He had a small pile of metal objects, rags, and a lighter. We placed our metal objects, towels, a gas can, and a few matches at his feet. "This should work" he said confidently.

He had us prepare some rags by dipping them into gasoline, and also had us rub some gasoline on the metal objects, letting the light dance across their polished metallic surfaces. After we had prepared everything, the warrior told us to get ready. We were going to set them ablaze, throw them out of the windows in front of the house, and then set the house itself on fire to create the ultimate distraction. The woman and I got excited at the formulation of the plan and agreed enthusiastically.

We gathered all of our supplies and went to the front of the house on the second floor. We began to set fire to the materials and throw them down the street. I could see a large crowd of infected in front of the house, trying to claw its way in. The front door was being broken through; we had to hurry.

More shrill cries were filling the air, making me tense. The fiery distractions caused about ten of the infected to follow them down the street, but many of them stayed, knowing they would get in and get to us eventually. "Now the house" the warrior said.

He walked calmly down the stairs, grabbing the gas can on his way down. The woman and I followed slowly, unsure of what he was about to do. He walked right up to the front door of the house, which was beginning to give way as the infected were edging their way through it. He slammed the gas can on the ground, causing gas to fly out of the can and coat everything with a thin layer of it. He turned his head towards us and said, "I guess it's time to heat things up", and tossed the lighter at the base of the front door.

The house began to go up in flames, coating everything with fire. The warrior walked back over to us, and the three of us stood there, watching the flames lick and feed themselves. The bright orange flames consumed whatever they touched, burning the house into submission.

The warrior spoke up, "Okay, let's get ready to make the climb down. I guarantee every one of those infected is coming to the front of the house as we speak." We began to walk up the stairs, but then a loud crash forced us to turn around.

I turned to see the infected knock the door down, releasing the flames pent up inside and also allowing them to come pouring in. Horrific screams of intense pain filled the house as the initial wave of infected was engulfed by the flames. More infected came flying in, knocking the others to the ground and heading right in our direction. I was the last one on the stairs, closest to their attack.

I began to pull my machete up to defend myself as they came upon me. I was knocked against the wall, trying to kick them to keep their vicious bites away from me. I managed to stick the blade of my machete against the throat of the main attacker. I slit its throat, letting its blood pour out onto my neck and chest.

Another one come from my right, grabbed my machete and threw it from me. I managed to pull my black pistol from my belt and put a bullet into that one and two others headed in my direction. More of them came flooding in, ready to taste my blood. I gave off a few more shots, ending my clip. I threw my gun down as they came towards me.

The next thing I saw was the warrior in front of me yelling, "Get out of here, I've got this!" He slew three infected with two blows from his axe, forcing blood to spout out of their bodies and coat the floor. The woman was gone, nowhere to be seen.

"Get out of here now!" he said, "It's your only chance!" I asked back as I quickly got to my feet, "What about you? I won't let you die!" He replied sharply, "I died a long time ago! Now get the hell out of here! Your girl is waiting for you! You can't die here!"

He said this as another wave of infected came through the door and straight at us. Everything in me told me to stay, to fight it out to the death, but I knew the warrior was right. I promised her I would not leave her alone; my little girl needed me to survive.

I yelled out in agony as I climbed the stairs, hating myself for leaving him to die. I ran up the stairs and picked up my bloody machete with one fell swoop. I sped through the hallway and into the bathroom, locking the door behind me. I came to the window; the warrior's plan had worked. There was not an infected to be seen.

I climbed out of the window and crossed the backyard, coming to the wall. I threw myself over the high brick wall, landing on my back on the opposite side. I got up and began to run through the forest.

Tears were streaming down my face as I ran through the forest. I ran for such a long time; I ran hard until I came to the hill we had seen on our way to Tuckerton.

I stood on the hill, looking at the godforsaken city. I watched the sunset, and I hated every second of it. The night would come and it would host a feast for those infected on the warrior. He would die in pain; maybe he already had. I watched until the sunset turned to night, allowing the stars to fill the sky. I cried as I walked slowly through the night to get back to the house.

After a seemingly endless amount of walking, I made it back to the house. I didn't want to go in; how could I face any of my companions? I sat down against the wall, next to the large metal doors.

I looked out into the night, questioning everything, hoping beyond all hope that the warrior and everyone else were still alive. The sky seemed to taunt me with its tranquility, revealing more of the chaos harboring in my heart.

After sitting there for quite some time, the doors opened up. I sat quietly as a group of my companions came walking out. The woman that had disappeared was walking alongside the red haired woman and her father. The red haired woman said, "But we have to go look for them. They're our friends!" The father replied, "It's too dangerous. We can't. We don't even know if any of them are still alive. They have to be dead by now for sure."

I stood up slowly, causing a stir. Four of the people in the group pointed guns at me, scared I could be an infected. I walked forward slowly and said, "I'm still alive." As soon as I had said this, the red haired woman ran up to me, embracing my tenderly. "Thank God!" she whispered in my ear.

"Are there any others with you that survived?" the father asked me. I shook my head with a solemn no. I could see pain in his eyes as he realized that the warrior, his good friend, did not make it back.

He shook it off, hiding his pain under his demanding presence. "Okay" he said; "Only six of your team made it back safely." He stopped short; he clenched his fists and looked down at the ground in front of him. The red haired woman walked back over to her father and placed her hands on his arm.

The man continued, "Why have we lost so many? It wasn't supposed to turn out this way. Is this all my fault?" He looked back up at me, meeting me with sorrowful eyes. "We lost most of our groups as well. Over half of us have been taken by those monsters. We're all that's left. We're all that's........." He stopped short.

He immediately pulled himself away from his daughter and walked briskly back into the large house in the midst of the base. The rest of us stood there in awe of the staggering losses we had suffered due to our operations in Tuckerton.

I just wanted to see my little girl; I walked away from the group and entered the house. I walked into the main entrance and dropped my pack on the floor. I had managed to keep it, preserving the items I had gathered earlier. I looked to my right, seeing the room of operations. A bunch of other packs were piled on the large table in that room. That gave me hope; at least we had salvaged something to keep us going. Maybe the deaths were not all meaningless and in vain.

I turned my attention forward and walked slowly and wearily up the stairs. I turned left and made my way down the hallway. I came to my door and put my ear to it; I could hear my little girl giggling as she talked with her older friend. I knocked weakly on the door.

As soon as the door opened, my little girl came flying into my arms. "You're back! You're back! I missed you!" she said as she embraced me tenderly. I walked over to the bed and held her in my arms. I held her in silence for a period of time. I kept thinking in my head. This little girl kept me going and I knew that I had to survive for her sake. She seemed to me a hope and a source of light, guiding me through the dark torrents of this time to a place where I could still find the sun smiling down on me.

After releasing her from my arms, I listened intently as she showed me her new drawings and told me of her adventures with her elderly friend. The older woman, sensing my tiredness, told her to go downstairs and let me get a chance to rest. I nodded thankfully as they left the room, closing the door behind them.

I lied down on my side, feeling sleep take me as I put my head on the pillow. Some tears escaped from my tired eyes as the world turned darkness around me.

I awoke to the high sun making its way through the window of my room. My body felt weary as I sat up in the bed. I rubbed my crusty eyes and let the world come into form around me.

I got out of bed and began to walk towards the door. The sound of rustling papers filled the still room as my feet spread some of the drawings that my little girl had left out. I went out into the hallway, walked to the right, and stopped at the top of the main stairs. I looked down into the main entrance, watching the people there for a moment; there were so few.

My mind flashed back to when the little girl and I first entered the base. I could see the raging river of people down below, the red haired woman in the midst of it, waiting for us to meet her.

Then I snapped into reality. The river had lost much of its water, only leaving the remnants of its previous existence amidst the small stream it left behind. A wave of anger swept over me as I thought on this. My hands gripped the banister in front of me tightly. I tried to choke the faded wood, crushing it under my hate until my knuckles turned white. So many were gone; every group that had been sent out had experienced staggering losses. We were all that was left.

I looked on in anger until the red haired woman came up behind me and placed her hand on my right shoulder. I looked over into her eyes. They were red and puffy, clear evidence that she had been lamenting over the loss of her friends as well as mine.

I asked her, "Are you all right?" She turned away from me, turning her attention to the main entrance as well. "No..." she said, "...and I don't think I will ever be." I turned my attention forward again as well, focusing on those words. How true they were; I could never be the same after what had happened.

We continued to stare off in silence until she turned to me and said, "I think we better go. We have to debrief everything with the other survivors in a few minutes." I gave her a solemn look and nodded slowly.

She got up and led the way down the stairs and into the operations room. We were the first ones there. All of the packs I had seen before were all gone; the supplies had probably been put away sometime earlier. We waited on until everyone else came to join us. The red haired woman's father was the last to come in.

He came in slowly, dragging his feet as he made his way to the nearest chair. He sat down heavily and looked around the room. Five chairs were empty, serving as reminders of the ones that had been lost. After some silence, he began the meeting.

He leaned forward and looked intently at everyone present. "Okay. Here's how it is: we were able to secure enough supplies to keep us going for a while, but they will only last so long. It will be much easier now that our numbers have decreased significantly." He paused before continuing on, looking for what he was trying to say.

He continued on, "We are not going to talk about the losses of our comrades; it's just too much right now. This is the main objective: survive. That is what we have to do; for ourselves and each other. There is no time for us to pity ourselves and allow grief to consume us. We need to come alongside each other and be the support to carry us on. We need to rely more heavily on each other, knowing we are incapable of doing this alone. We will take a few days to situate ourselves, then we have to begin operations once again.

I know; none of you want to go back out there knowing those demons are on the prowl, hungry for our flesh. But we have to; we just have to. Take the next few days to find closure, rest, and get ready for new operations. Mend your broken hearts, because that's what is essential to where we are right now."

Tears were beginning to well up in his eyes as he said all of these things. As I listened closely, hanging on to every word out of his mouth, I could feel tears running down my face. I looked around the room; everyone else in the room was crying, doing their best to keep composure.

No dry eyes at all; I could see the pain writhing about in our hearts, trying to infect us and kill us off, like some sort of disease. I turned back to the father as he said his last words. "That's all there is to it; that's all I have to..."

He could not let the words find their way out of his mouth. His bottom lip started to quiver as tears rolled down his cheeks. He pulled a pipe out with his shaking hands and struggled to light up what had been placed inside of it. He got up, trying to take a puff to console himself. His lips were shaking intensely as he tried to puff; the pipe fell out of his mouth and landed in his hands. The father immediately turned away from us and walked into the main entrance. We all watched on, seeing how deep the anguish of his heart was.

He stopped, looking down at the pipe in his hands. He stood there for a few moments, probably reminiscing about his good friend the warrior. Then he raised his hands high and smashed the pipe on the ground, filling the room with the sounds of the crash. Pieces of it flew everywhere, coating the floor with destruction. He stamped out the lit herbs on the floor, and walked briskly out of the house.

After that, those of us left looked down into our hands, looking for something that was never really there. Everyone slowly trickled out, until the room lay completely empty. We spent the next few days consoling ourselves and getting ready for the next round of survival; I think we knew it would be the hardest time of our lives before it even began.

TAPE #11

Operations began again after those few days of rest. The red haired woman's father began to expand operations, telling us we needed to venture farther out into the surrounding areas. We were to stick to small areas and towns, completely avoiding any main cities; they were too dangerous.

Many, including myself and the red haired woman, were reluctant to venture out again, especially after witnessing the hell that broke out in Tuckerton. I found out that the she and I had experienced the most losses in our groups. Less than half of each group had been able to survive. Yet, we were able to continue on with the missions afforded us, bringing back enough to help keep everyone going for days at a time.

A long and fluid stream of months passed. The continued fight for survival intensified as the supplies around us began to dwindle, but still we made due. Those of us that remained became a close-knit community. We began to rely on each other and stick close together.

The red haired woman and I would go on walks every few days or so, talking about our lives, our hopes and dreams, and what we imagined ourselves doing if the outbreak had never occurred.

She had imagined herself as a prominent nurse working in a major hospital. She would be saving lives every day, giving hope to the broken, and following in her mother's footsteps. She even imagined that she would be working underneath her mother, allowing them to form the most dynamic duo ever to hit the nursing world. She would come up with all sorts of scenarios that would involve her saving lives just in the nick of time. She told me she liked the most intense stories better, like the ones involving pulling a person back from the brink of death, because the differences she saw there were greater than that of a pure and simple encounter.

She said that people were more likely to transform and change their lives when they seemed to have lost everything and then are able to come back to salvage them. The red haired woman was adamant about these life and death scenarios because they would put her to the test as well.

She told me she could see her mother and herself pouring through countless medical journals and research in order to find ways to conquer incurable diseases that devastated a person. Racing against the clock, holding death in the left hand and life in the right, nobody could really tell which way it would go. However, despite all odds, they would be able to do it; the impossible.

I admired her dreams. She was able to keep such a deep-seeded hope that could help her carry on the memory of her mother while remaining firm in herself as well. I also pondered what I would have been doing if the hell we knew now had never happened.

I saw myself as a janitor for two or three more years, scraping by to find a place that would welcome me in to work at my desired profession as a lawyer. I would be with my wife and child, maybe with another one on the way. Scraps would be getting bigger, causing more havoc as he trashed the house while having all of us rolling on the floor with laughter.

I could see my child, either as a boy or a girl. Either way, it would be our child; it would be the accumulation of our joy, our love, our pain, and our undying commitment to each other.

I could see my boy; he would grow up well, taking after me in his nature, but retaining so many of my wife's delicate yet sturdy features. He would be a sports-minded person that was able to balance that nature well with his academics. He would grow up to be someone important, like a CEO of a company or something. He would use all of his resources for the greater good, making his parents proud.

I could see the other side as a girl. She would take after her mother, but would have some of the harder features of my body. She would be sassy, but would be able to show unbelievable depth through compassion and empathy. She would want to live a simple lifestyle as a teacher, just like her wondrous mother. She would raise up the next generation through teaching, creating an environment that would allow the children to grow and flourish.

Above all, I saw my life with my beautiful wife. We would be so happy; we would love each other so much. I would be content to lie in her arms, letting her stroke my hair with her light caresses. I would be honored to wake up in the morning way before she did to make her a breakfast in bed and bad coffee that always needed more creamer to be tolerable.

We would go on long walks, simply dwelling in each other's presence. I would come from work back to the house and get dinner cooked and ready for when she would return from a long day of teaching. She would be the queen of my life; she would be my better half, my soul.

I could see that life that had left me so long ago when she died; when she was ripped out of my life by bitter circumstance and the downward spiral of society due to the outbreak. It was nice to imagine, but it carried some traces of still fresh pain. It hurt to think these things, but it helped me cope.

I wanted to be naïve, to convince myself that in some other dimension in some other world we could be happy together. I wanted to believe that there was still hope, even though it never existed in the first place.

I also thought of the future of my little girl that was at the base. If all of this had not happened, I could see where she would have ended up. She would have been able to be happy with her mother and father. I could see her growing up well in school, playing soccer in her spare time. She would have a natural affinity for artistic expression, creating impressive pieces that would reflect her heart in the world. She would be excelling in every area of her life due to her own drive and the undying support of her loving parents. I made myself so sad pondering how she would have been able to grow up into a beautiful and amazing woman. Her father would cry tears of joy as her walked her down the aisle to the man of her dreams on her wedding day. Then she would live in her happily ever after, or at least as close to it as she could possible get.

But all of these futures had been cast aside and destroyed by the reality before us. We would have to forsake what could have been for the real and horrible present gnawing away at our hopes and dreams.

In all reality, these walks and thoughts were a great release. I could allow myself to let loose some of what had been eating me up inside. Giving presence to the loss of my family allowed the giant infected hole in my heart to grow slightly smaller; not by much, but still, it grew that much smaller.

The operations that we were required to perform became more and more tedious as they were expanded. We had to travel farther out into areas that would take almost a whole day to reach. At the same time, the resources that we were able to find were only able to keep us going for days at a time. It seemed pointless to go and scavenge for such menial supplies, but we had to do it in order to survive.

Since an operation would take about two and a half days round trip, the groups that were sent out were able to grow closer. Even the most socially awkward of us opened up. It wasn't because of some magical family dynamic or anything; it was mostly due to the fact that we were all afraid of the dark.

The dark is where the shadows were; the dark is where the infected thrived. I had heard and seen many instances over that period of time of this fact. During most of our missions, the infected stuck to coming after us at night. They would always strike in the middle of the night, under the deep cloak of darkness. They truly were animals; they knew how to hunt us and find us wherever we were.

Operations became a thing to be feared, not anything to feel obligated to help serve others by. At the same time, my own fear of the dark had increased by a thousand times due to the nightmare I had been having.

The same dream had been recurring in my mind over and over again every few nights. I never knew when it would come; it would happen at random intervals of time whenever I slept.

It always started out the same: I would be in complete darkness as a cold fear began to sweep over my entire being. I would look in all directions to find no hope in sight. In the complete darkness I could feel something watching me, hunting me, thirsting for me. Then I would run; I would break out into a full on sprint, trying to escape the unknown thing coming after me. I felt like I didn't make any progress as I could only find more darkness to run to.

All of a sudden, my feet would be thrown out from under me and I would fall face first onto the ground. I would hit it hard, which caused me to close my eyes and allowed me to taste the warm blood filling my mouth.

After I got up, the darkness before me was illuminated with a brilliant and bright starry night sky. I would be reminded of being home at the base, being able to see every interstellar connection between each extraterrestrial body.

I would look around me to find myself in the middle of an endless field of waist-high grass. It would sway in an invisible and untouchable breeze, inviting me to walk through it. I would still have an uneasy feeling in the back of my mind, causing all of my hair to stand on end. That told me to keep moving and never stop.

I would walk through the field gazing at the stars, trying to keep myself from looking behind me. Everything inside told me not to look back; it would mean certain death.

After walking for some time, I would come across my home. Not the base, but the house I had lived in prior to the outbreak. It would be in unnaturally good condition, given that everything was in a severe state of decay due to the flow of time. The disturbing feeling would drive me on towards the house as the house itself beckoned me into its haven.

By this time, I would have a cold sweat all over my body in fear of what was to come. There was just some ominous feeling that was causing my heart to hurt. The pain of my face hitting the ground would subside. I would make my way onto the porch, heading towards the door. I always stopped when my hand turned the doorknob.

A sensation of pain and regret would shoot through my heart, paralyzing me for a second. As I stood there paralyzed I could feel it; it was breathing in my ear, filling my body with hate, disgust, and fear at the same time.

Then, in one quick movement, I would throw the door open, step inside, and close it behind me, locking the door. I would fall to the ground breathing heavily, evidence of a close call. Then I would get up and step into the middle of an empty house. There was no furniture on the first floor as I walked around, wondering where everyone was. After surveying the first floor, I would make my way to the second. There is where everything always went wrong.

I would ascend the stairs slowly, getting another uneasy feeling with every step. I would reach the top of the stairs and look around. The first thing I always saw was the trail of blood. It came out of nowhere. I would look down on the floor, seeing a thick, fresh blood trail leading from downstairs and into my bedroom.

I would get sick to the stomach, fearful of what monster could have done such a thing. Then I would look around again. Four doors: one to the nursery, one to the bathroom, one to a closet, and one to my room.

I always walked down the hall to my room, never skipping a beat. The door was locked. I would put my ear against it; nothing. Then I would try to pry it open. After a few failed attempts, I kicked the door in with all my might. It always opened to a horrific crime scene.

I would see a woman on the floor, holding a child. Next to their bodies was the corpse of a dog. I walked over to them and scanned their bodies. The dog had been chewed through at the neck, showing that the spine was the only thing still connecting head to body in its large pool of blood. The collar had a shine to it, allowing me to see the name of the dog; it was Scraps.

Tears would begin to well up in my eyes as I turned from Scraps to the other bodies. Every time, I hoped it wasn't them; every time, I was completely crushed.

The bodies were no doubt those of my wife and child. My child's corpse would be missing its head as blood was spurting out if its neck. The corpse of my wife would be cradling the child deep into her chest in her lifeless arms. She had deep scratches on her neck that were bleeding out. At the same time, she would be eaten through at the chest, allowing me to see her broken heart in the gaping chest cavity.

The floor was completely covered in thick, slimy blood. Tears would flow heavily down my face as I took in the scene. I got on my knees, bringing the corpses closer.

In the midst of my suffering I could hear footsteps. They were dull and heavy at first, but they became louder with every step. Something was inside the house! I would turn around, looking intently at the dark and empty corridor from the room. The footsteps got louder and louder, banging against the floors of the house. They seemed to pierce through the walls, echoing in my head.

Paralyzing fear gripped me as I could sense the demonic presence of the unknown. I looked into the darkness, hoping to see my enemy. All of a sudden, two evil white eyes would flash open and reveal a nasty wide grin beneath them. Its teeth were yellow and mangy, with green slime dripping from them. I couldn't move; everything inside of me kept me pinned to the ground. It would always step slowly out of the darkness, rising up and facing me. The dim light of the room allowed me to see the figure more clearly.

How was my face over there? How could that even be possible? Yet, it was there; it was my face and my body, completely recognizable underneath the decay of the rabid infection. I was the enemy, I was the creature, I was the monster! He stepped forth heavily, right up to my face. He would have a disgusting smile spreading from ear to ear, taunting me. He leaned in so close I could have reached out to feel his decaying flesh. Then he let out a scream that made everything within me explode; it filled the room, the house, and the very crevices of my heart with suffering. Then he leaned back, rose up high, opened his mouth, and swallowed me whole.

That's when I woke up every time. The first few times scared those who were with me as I awoke with a terrified and painful scream, but then I got used to it. I would wake up with a small whimper and in a cold sweat. Everyone in the group got used to it after I was able to adjust to the dream. Still, the red haired woman worried about me.

I would always tell her that I was fine, but she and I knew that I truly wasn't. Naturally, I would be the one to volunteer to guard our group through the night. I was too scared to sleep; it hurt my heart too much to try.

As we neared the end of our ropes, forcing us to travel even farther out into deep areas of the country for anything that would allow us to survive just that much longer, the presence of the infected began to grow. They began to get desperate, attacking the venturing groups multiple times in one night. As we were able to fend them off, they would still impatiently wait for us in the darkness, looking for a moment of weakness in order to strike.

Missions began to be extremely tedious, forcing the groups sent out to travel for days at a time to make it to the objective destination and back. We had a few casualties, and some came back with nothing of true value to us, which began to cause a panic. We began to institute the usual measures of a crisis situation: we had to ration our food, lock down at the base as soon as it began to get dark, and post a watch at night just for good measure.

The base that seemed like a home for this long had turned into some sort of prison. It actually made me a little glad to leave the base on missions because I could get a little freedom from this kind of confinement. Everyone else seemed content with it, hoping to return from a mission as soon as possible back to the false security of the base.

Time passed under this regime, and all of our resources were beginning to dwindle into nothing. In desperation, the red haired woman's father created a last ditch effort to find something, if anything, to give us enough time to find out a plan for everyone to survive. Late one night, he called a meeting of all the manpower we had left; everyone was to play a role in this desperate operation.

As soon as everyone had gathered in the common area in the midst of the house, the red haired woman's father ascended the stairs before us and spoke from the banister above us. He went through this long dissertation about our current situation: we were a lot of manpower short, our supplies were almost completely drained, the infected were becoming more and more aggressive, venturing nearer to our base every single day, and all the rest of the reality we all already knew. After reminding us of the current predicament we were in, he began to speak of a place that we could go. A few days travel away was a large bridge connecting two small cities. His plan was for all of the remaining manpower, save a few to remain behind to guard the others, to go to this place and find anything, if anything, for us to keep going. He finished by saying, "This is our last and final option; we don't have any choice left."

He stopped and let the silence creep into the room. Everyone looked around, looking for someone to speak up and agree to the mission that could so easily go wrong. After some more awkward silence, he spoke up. The red haired woman's father aimed his statement at me, calling me out by name. All eyes turned on my as he yelled out, "Well? What do you have to say? Will you go with me, or will you be a coward and let all of us die out in here? You've carried out so many successful missions, and you would still sit idly by and let the infected take us all out as soon as we had nothing left? Are you that weak and scared? You can help sway all of these people here! Even my own daughter would not go! Well? What do you have to say? Speak up!"

I froze. I met his angry gaze from the floor below. I could feel the tension in the room, like a heavy weight that had been placed on my shoulders. His eyes were flared up in anger, demanding me to be the one to turn the tables of cowardice. I looked into myself, trying to find out what I truly wanted to do. I was so fearful of going out to a place that could end up like Tuckerton again. I didn't want to think about any more deaths, let alone my own. It was a close call back then; I could definitely not afford another one.

I thought of my little girl; I had to keep my promise at all costs, no matter what. I kept searching, deep into my own fears, trying to muster up the courage to go.

I thought about it deeply, weighing both options. If we went, we would likely die, leaving everyone to fend for themselves at the hands of the infected. If it did go well, we would barely be able to survive for another few days, putting us in the same place as we were in at this moment. If we did not go, then we would run out of supplies and die out and look for desperate measures of survival. Either way, we were all completely screwed! I continued to deliberate on both options as anxiety filled my body.

How could such a choice be put on me? Why did I have to be the one to hold everyone's lives in their hands? As I continued to think, I saw something upstairs.

In the dim light of the house, I could see my little girl coming out from the hallway, holding her ragged teddy bear tightly in her arms. She looked so innocent and beautiful in the dim light of the room. I took a long look at her, realizing just how much she had grown.

She was tall now, at least tall enough to reach my neck by only being on her toes. Her hair was getting so long; it was in a long braid that reached down to the midline of her back, signifying how much time had passed over the years.

She was pencil thin, resembling a thin spruce tree that wavered under the wind of a coming storm. Her clothes barely fit her; It was a wonder that she was able to find another purple jacket that kept her from looking like a tree in too small of clothes. It resembled the first, puffiness and all. Her jeans only reached just above her ankles, and her worn shoes revealed her small, delicate toes that were supposed to be hidden beneath the lacing. Her ragged teddy bear had deteriorated heavily, requiring various emergency stitchings and stuffings in order for it to reach its next day of life.

I felt warmed by her presence; as if a small light had been placed in my hands whose rays of calm radiated through my body, down to my core. I lost myself in this momentary joy, forgetting the immense weight that was laid upon my shoulders. I dwelt in it for another minute, slowly letting myself slip back into reality.

Then it hit me full force; the room took shape once again before my eyes, and the unbearable weight felt even heavier upon my shoulders. I took another quick glance at my little girl, and all was lost. I didn't want to die some place far away from her, from the red haired woman, from everyone that was there in our makeshift family; I just wanted to die with the ones I loved.

Maybe I was a coward, maybe I was weak. At least I knew I was weak enough to trust in those around me and wish to end my days in their company. My heart caved in, and I gave my answer.

"N-n-no" I said weakly, stuttering as the word formed itself on my lips and let itself loose into the room. I was shocked as I said it, but it let the weight slip right off of my shoulders, falling limp on the ground behind me.

"What did he say?" a few of them murmured, wanting to know my final decision. The word gained force, coming out once again. "No" I said louder, allowing it to sink into the crowd. The red haired woman's father called out angrily, "Well, what is your answer? Speak up!"

I replied with strength, yelling it out. It took a second for him to register after it had reached his ears. The crowd between us remained silent, acting as a useless blockade to keep him from reaching me. He said nothing; he simply walked towards the staircase and proceeded down. I focused my eyes on my little girl as fear crept over me. I did not want to see him as he came in my direction.

All at once I could feel him; a cold presence crept up my spine as his hot breath hit me right in the face. I took my eyes off of my little girl and met his gaze. His eyes were flared up in anger so intense it looked as if volcanoes were erupting in his head.

"Say it again" he said, making his body even larger in front of me. "No" I said weakly, unsure of what to say.

I continued, "If we're going to die either way, I at least want to die here with my family and not in some unknown place due to a futile mission. That's my decision, as selfish as it sounds to you. You may think I'm a coward, but at least I know what I want, and what everyone else really wants too."

He pushed me; I landed hard on the wooden surface of the floor, sliding away and creating a good distance between us. The crowd around us protested him, agreeing that I was right.

However, they stepped away from us, forming a ring to trap us in the middle of the room. I knew what was going to happen; we were going to have to fight it out to truly determine the next course of action. Everyone reaffirmed that they agreed with me, but I could see that they still respected and feared the red haired woman's father.

I stood slowly and tensed up, expecting him to charge me. Instead, he walked slowly and fiercely up to me, grabbing the collar of my shirt. He raised his right fist high, preparing for a blow to my face. He never got to finish the job.

There was a loud bang on the door. Then it turned into a banging that shook the entire room. Everyone stopped and focused intently on the door. The banging gained force, filling the entire house with its noise. The red haired woman's father changed his expression from one of anger to one of curiosity.

"What could that be?" he murmured to himself as he released me and began to move away. He walked towards the door, seeing the worried looks on peoples' faces. "Don't worry. We'll see what it is. It's probably nothing." He said as he made his way through the crowd and headed towards the door. I could see that he was shaking slightly. A pit began to form in my stomach; something was not right.

The crowd of people came behind me, leaving me at the head of it. The red haired woman came beside me, handing me my machete and a gun. I looked into her anxious eyes as I received them. "I'm scared" she said, "Something's going to happen."

I didn't respond as the pit began to grow heavy in my stomach. I took a quick glance at the crowd, seeing that some had armed themselves, just in case. I turned my attention, alongside everyone else, to the red haired woman's father.

He began to shake heavily, placing his hand on the pounding door. I could see that he had a shiny metal pipe in his right hand; he could sense it too. We all drew breath as he grabbed the handle and began to open the door.

It truly was a flood; as soon as he had opened the door, it seemed to fly off of its hinges. An outpour of infected, at least twenty, came rushing in, crushing the man under the weight of the door. They flew right at the crowd. They were met with a shower of bullets. Most of them were knocked down onto the floor, writhing as they let out dying shrieks.

A few came leaping into the crowd, attacking us. I managed to slit one open from its chin down to its legs as it tried to leap above me. Its thick, cudgeled blood showered the floor as it made its way to the ground behind me.

I got a look at the door as more infected came rushing in. I could see past them, out into the main ground. The grounds were covered with infected, resembling frenzied ants on an ant hill. They were running to and fro as many headed in our direction.

The second rush came in and was met with a smaller shower of bullets. At least another group of twenty came pouring in, a few of them being knocked to the side by the red haired woman's father, who had gotten out from underneath the door and was fighting as well.

This next group came flying right into us, knocking those next to me back and onto the floor as we tried to fight them off. I pulled out my pistol and took two or three of them out. One large infected tackled me down to the floor, knocking my pistol out of my hand. In one fluid motion, I pulled out my machete and stuck it into the center of its head. It fell to the side as I pulled my blade out and got up. I was greeted with three more infected charging in my direction. I clenched my fist tightly around the handle of my weapon and charged at them.

I met them head on, slashing one across the stomach, slicing another across the neck, and tackling the third one to the floor. I hit it in the center of its chest, knocking it down onto the floor. I quickly got up and stamped my foot directly into its face. It let out a muffled squeal under the weight of my body.

One of the trio came up next to me, trying to attack from my right. I fought it off with my machete, inflicting large gashes across its frail arms. I continued to stomp hard on the face of the infected on the floor until it went limp. My shoe began to feel wet and slimy as I continued to stomp with all of my might onto the face of the hideous creature.

The final infected came from my left side, grabbing my arm. I turned quickly in its direction and kicked it between the legs with force. It let out a painful shriek as it staggered back a few steps.

I focused on the infected to my right; I found an opportunity to strike, slashing my blade across its neck, causing blood to spray from its throat. The blood sprayed the floor and coated my arm. I quickly spun around, but not quickly enough. The final infected shoved me, lifting me off of my feet and causing me to land hard against a nearby wall. It charged me as I tried to gather myself. I stuck my blade out in front of my face; the infected ran right into it. Its face was so close to mine I could have kissed it.

I could see its disgusting face; it was covered in bloody and cracked skin. Thick green pus was flowing from its nostrils. It had almost no hair, save a few strands covering its hateful face. Its mouth revealed black gums and vibrant yellow teeth. Bloody saliva filled its mouth, running down the blade and landing on my chest. The blade had pierced through its head, exiting out of the backside. It tried to bite me, pushing itself deeper into the blade and trying to close its dying mouth. It was a few centimeters from my face as it coughed. Its saliva filled blood was spat all over my face. After another moment, it died. I turned over, pulling my blade out and wiping my face.

I took a quick look around the room; it was filled with more infected trying to fight their way to us. I saw a few of my comrades in the center of the room being eaten away by multiple infected.

They ate like animals. They were biting down hard, ripping their flesh from my friends' bodies. Blood and tissue were flying everywhere, coating the floor and the infected horde. I turned away as I saw them pulling out and biting down on the intestines of a woman I had once known.

I felt a hand on my shoulder and turned around swiftly; it was the red haired woman's father. He grabbed my arm while saying, "Let's go! We have to get upstairs where we can get them in tighter spaces!"

My mind immediately flashed to my little girl. Where was she? She could be hurt! I asked hurriedly, "Where's my little girl? She needs to be safe!" He replied, "Don't worry! My daughter has her! They're hiding out in the attic with a few others! The infected can't reach them there! Hurry, let's go!"

I followed him up the stairs as infected followed close behind. As soon as we reached the top, the red haired woman's father threw me on the ground and dove on top of me. I covered my head as bullets flew over us, nailing the large group of infected behind us head on. Their shrieks filled the air as their bodies tumbled down the stairs. The red haired woman's father pulled me up onto my feet, facing the stairs.

I prepared my machete as I saw another group of infected barging through the door. My body felt heavy as I could feel the weariness of battle. A group of six of us charged down the stairs at the oncoming infected, knocking them back as we sped down.

I leaped into the air at the oncoming group, slicing one across the face and kicking another one hard with both of my feet. I tumbled down the stairs, taking six or seven of them with me. I hit the ground and rolled to my feet.

I took a second to survey the chaos; there were less infected in the house, about thirty. They were spread across it in groups of five or six as they ransacked the house. It seemed like they were losing interest in attacking us for now because we were hitting them with significant losses.

I stuck my blade through the skull of an infected as the other men joined me. I told them to go stop the other groups of infected around the house as I spotted my pistol a little ways away on the ground, just behind a group of infected that were eating one of the carcasses of my fallen comrades. They finished killing off the infected lying in a heap at the bottom of the stairs as I began to make my way over to my pistol.

Blood was spreading across the floor, soaking into the wooden floorboards. The bodies of countless infected lay strewn across the ground, creating a maze of bodies on the floor. I began to step over the bodies, making my way to the pistol.

I came into an arm's length of my pistol and reached for it. As I grabbed it, I felt a hard pull on my ankle that caused me to slip on the bloody floor onto my back. I turned as a bloody infected jumped onto my chest, letting its saliva fly onto my face. I pulled my pistol up to its forehead and let two shots fill the air. Its head exploded as the body fell on the floor next to me.

I quickly turned onto my knees and looked back at the group of infected before me. Four of them had turned around, facing me with hungry and angry eyes. I pulled my pistol before me and let the last two shots of my clip hit two of the infected dead on. The other two leaped into the air at me, their teeth bared. I pulled my arms up to my face as I realized I had let go of my machete to grab my gun.

The whole scene seemed to go in slow-motion: as I watched the two infected leaping at me, I could see the red haired woman's father running in from the far field of my vision. He dove into the air, leaping in front of me.

One of the infected took a bite right out of his arm and the other dove into his chest as they hit the ground hard nearby. He kicked and hit the infected with his metal pipe as they combated on the floor.

I quickly got to my feet, grabbed my fallen machete, and headed over to their fight. I slashed one of infected across the back, causing it to rear up and allowing the father to put his metal pipe right through its head.

Then he kicked the other one away from us, knocking it hard against the wall. I ran over to it and slit its throat. It attempted to shriek, but choked on the blood rising into its throat, suppressing its cry. I saw the life leave its body as it gasped for air and limply fell to the floor.

I ran back over to the red haired woman's father; he was sitting against the doorway leading into the open living area, which was filled with more bodies. I saw that the infected had cleared out and the remaining men had begun to seal up the doors to the house. I could hear muffled shrieks fading from hearing as the red haired woman's father pulled me in close.

He was fading fast as the infection was beginning to course its way through his veins. The first thing I saw was the gaping wound on his left forearm. The wound was bleeding profusely down his arm and onto the floor. The veins surrounding his arm and neck were turning black as the poison was spreading rapidly through his body.

I looked into the blue-green eyes in his pale face. He motioned for me to come closer with his right hand. He was coughing up blood as he whispered quietly, "I'm sorry...I see what you were saying...about...not leaving. Please keep my...daughter...and everyone else...safe. It's up to...you...now. This isn't....your fault; it would have...happened anyway.

You need to survive...and keep moving. You can't stay here.......anymore. It's not safe. I........."

He never got to finish telling me his last words. Heavy tears flowed down my face as I pulled myself away from his cold body. He had a calmer expression on his face based on the gravity of all that had happened; maybe he knew he was going to see his wife.

I looked around at the men; they were watching me wipe the tears from my eyes. I turned to them and said, "Let's start clearing out the bodies. We have to prepare in case they try to attack us again."

They slowly turned their attention from me and the body of the red haired woman's father and began to take the bodies outside. I told them to leave his body at least until the red haired woman could see it for herself.

I helped clear some of the bodies, forming a large pile outside the house. I could see that the infected had somehow opened the steel doors isolating the base from the outside world. It was covered in blood; the surrounding wall had blood splashed across it at all angles, signifying the struggle our outside guards put up as they tried to dam the flood of infected.

I walked back into the house and up the main staircase. I found the entrance to the attic and pulled the ladder down. I ascended it and looked into the dark room. I was met with pistol pressed against my forehead. I quickly stated, "It's all right. The fighting's over. You guys can come out now."

The pistol was pulled away and I descended the ladder. Everyone that had been hiding up there, about eight people, came down with the red haired woman leading the way.

My little girl came up to me; she had tears in her eyes and looked afraid. I reached out to hold her, but she backed away into the red haired woman. "You're covered in blood," the red haired woman said.

I looked down at my body, which was covered in fresh blood all over. I looked back up at her and asked her to escort my little girl to her room to wait for me to get cleaned up. As the two of them stepped away, I grabbed the red haired woman's arm to hold her back for a second. She quickly turned and faced me, wondering what I wanted. I gave her an extremely worried look as I shook my head. She understood immediately and said, "You wait here; I need to see him."

I nodded and stayed glued to my spot. She took my little girl to the room and returned momentarily. She came up to me, grabbed my hand, and said, "Show me." Tears were welling up in her eyes as I looked into their deep blue oceans. I held her hand tightly and led her downstairs to her father's body.

As soon as the body came into view, she let out a horrified scream as she pulled herself away from me and ran to the body. She cried in the midst of her grieving shrieks as she cradled the body of her dead father. I watched on painfully as she did so until her voice was hoarse and she could no longer cry.

After the red haired woman had finished lamenting over her dead father, I told some men to take the body outside with the others and then I helped her to her room. She limply sat onto her bed and stared off into the night sky outside. I watched her staring off in the distance and waited for a response. After a few minutes of waiting, she finally said, "Please, just go. Good night."

I left her room slowly and silently, closing the door behind me. I walked down the hall to the washroom and ran the water. The weak stream of water was just enough for me to wash off the dried blood that was caked all over my face and arms. I watched solemnly as the blood filled the rusty sink basin and flowed into the drain.

How many innocent lives were in that blood? How many souls were filling the sink in front of me, going down the drain to be forgotten just like that? How could they have known or wanted to become the evil creatures outside? The innocent had to be taken away alongside the guilty as no justice reigned at all? I looked up into the broken mirror in front of me as I thought on this. I could see my shattered reflection revealing various images of who I was.

Which one was the real me? They all looked so weary, as if I would cave in on myself at any second. My eyes were red from crying and my face had aged beyond belief. I could see the cuts I had on me that were still bleeding, mixing with the blood that had caked itself onto my skin. I didn't want to look at myself any longer; I finished washing and left the room, making my way down to my bedroom where my little girl was waiting for me.

I stopped at the door; I took a second to look at the large flower spanning the length of the door. It was a gigantic blue rose with yellow on the tips of the petals. It was in the midst of blooming, and a sun was beginning to protrude out of its center. The stem of the flower curved to the base of the door. Large thorns aligned themselves along the stem, protecting it from any harm. A few small leaves were budding out of the stem, casting some shadows upon the base of the flower. I spent a few moments looking at the flower, and then I opened the door.

My little girl was sound asleep, clutching her ragged teddy bear for dear life on top of the covers. I watched her sleep for a few minutes, seeing the worry on her face. I stepped back and saw the chair at the base of the window nearby. She did not stir as I made my way to the chair facing out into the night sky. The chair creaked as I fell into it. I looked back to make sure I did not wake her. She didn't stir from my presence in the room. I turned back to the window and stared out into the star-streaked sky, wondering how light and beauty could still be present amidst all the ugliness going on.

I could see a large cloud cover coming in over the mountains in the far right side of the view I had; it had not rained for a long time in our area. That gave me some comfort, but in all reality I knew it could only be a foreshadowing of worse things that were to come. I watched the storm clouds move in closer as the deep weight of sleep came over me.

TAPE #12

Thankfully the attack did not reduce our numbers drastically; nine of us had not made it through. However, each individual loss carried great weight to all of us.

The death of the red haired woman's father, the leader of our company, hit everyone especially hard. It hit the red haired woman and me the hardest of all.

We decided to hold a funeral for those who died that night, letting everyone have a turn to say their goodbyes and give their eulogies. It lasted for about an hour, and the whole service ended with the burning of the bodies. We burned our dead separately from the dead infected, creating two burning heaps that allowed pillars of smoke to form, creating a bridge from the earth to the heavens.

After the funeral, we collectively called a gathering in the main entrance of the house. People seemed nervous standing in that space, looking around in grief at the dried bloody streaks covering the house from top to bottom. We all knew what had to be done: we needed to elect a new leader to give us a purpose and a direction.

An older man in our group announced why we were all together, and who the three candidates for leadership were. It came down to three men: the older man doing the announcing, a younger man who had proved himself worthy through his intelligence, prowess, and countless successful missions, and me. Surprisingly, the vote was unanimous.

It was a little slow at first as the hands trickled up in vote of me, but soon the whole room, even the other candidates, had their hands raised collectively in favor of me. I felt heavy as I left the hands of my little girl and the red haired woman and ascended the stairs. With each step upwards, I felt an invisible weight on my shoulders get heavier, digging into my back and pushing down on me with all its might.

I did, however, feels some sort of responsibility and honor. I wondered: is this what the red haired woman's father had felt every second of every day? Is this what holding lives in the balance with every move and decision you make feels like? How would I know what the right thing to do was?

I was so scared to fail them. I was afraid that I would make the decision that would either lead us to safety or have all of us die at the hands of the infected, or worse, each other.

I made it to the top of the stairs and came up to the banister overlooking the crowd. I stared silently at every one of them, hoping that I could find words to say, but I had none.

After a few minutes of silence, a woman at the edge of the group shouted, "Well, what are you going to do? Where are we going to go?" Another few began to question me, wondering what I would do to find us a place that ensured our survival. I looked down at the red haired woman; she was holding my little girl tight against her side, looking up at me with fearful and curious eyes as well.

I quickly took everything into account before I would make a decision. We were running out of supplies, we had drained all of the areas nearby and faraway of anything useful to keep us going, the infected were on the move, inching closer and closer to our necks every day, our group only numbered twenty-two, we had lost our leader, and the only way to escape this hell and possibly end up in another one was the blockade that had been set up at the beginning of the infection, isolating us in the area as the infected took it over and retained dominion over it. We had no options, and worse of all, no hope.

I stood there frozen for a minute or so, taking all of these factors into account. I knew there was nowhere we could go in our area where the infected couldn't reach us and that we could find adequate supplies in, but it would be a suicide mission to try to make it through the blockade, which seemed to be endless as it separated us from the rest of civilization. I had scouted it out before with a group in search of supplies, and we almost lost our lives doing it. I remember it well.

It was a secret mission that the red haired woman's father had sent us on, lying to everyone else that it was just a last ditch search for supplies in an area we had already scoured and stripped clean. I was with a group of seven others, and we were sent to see how bad the blockade had gotten after Tuckerton.

We made it there under the cloak of night, ensuring some chance of passing through unseen. We made it to the base of the blockade's high walls and threw ourselves over. We landed softly on the grass and made our way past a large series of chain linked fences that were laced with barbed wire all around. After these there was an open space for a mile or so that was filled with decomposed dead bodies and various military vehicles. It resembled a battleground as blood covered the light brown soil and the sides of the vehicles; it was a mix of infected and soldiers' bodies, each toppled over each other.

I looked to my left and right; the blockade spanned on endlessly in both directions, continuing on out of my range of sight. I imagined that it separated the whole world from us, permanently closing us off from the rest of civilization.

After this there was a high metal wall with various holes in it. I could see some gun nozzles poking out from some of the holes; perhaps it had been some last line of defense for the humans against the infected. It apparently had not held. There were two humongous metal doors that produced an entrance into the dark facility before us. We turned on some flashlights and hesitantly entered the darkened facility.

Once inside, we could only navigate through by the light of our flashlights and the places where the night sky penetrated through some tears within the metal frame above us.

It was dangerously quiet; the only sounds that echoed through the metal halls were our own footsteps. As we scanned the passing walls, one of my teammates was able to locate a map of the facility embedded on the ground of one of the rooms connected to a nearby hallway. We took a second to look it over, taking in the enormity of the complex.

In the upper right corner of the map there was a scale of how big the complex was. We estimated that it was six miles across, if one were to run straight through it. I took a few pieces of paper and used the map to embed its image on each piece. I numbered them to make sure we could replicate the image of the complex accurately.

I noticed that there were various side hallways that could also achieve the journey from one side of the facility to the other; it would just take a longer amount of time. After taking down the images of the map we moved on through the facility.

We navigated our way through various piles of debris, some preventing us from going straight forward, forcing us to use some of the side hallways. After taking a large series of hallways to avoid a large pile of the destruction on the main path, we ended up back on our original trajectory.

We walked along the steel grating on the floor, being careful not to make too much noise. After quietly moving along for some time, we could see the other side far off in the distance. I knew it was the other side because I could see a small slit in the wall from top to bottom, letting out into the night sky outside. We continued towards it, making sure to stay cautious.

Of course I had to be the one that botched the mission. I heard a slight breath that seemed a little out of place on my far left side. I had everyone turn off their flashlights and I immediately focused my flashlight in the direction of the sound. I took a quick glance and immediately covered the light in my hand. I saw two infected standing together, crouching as they faced the wall away from us. I prayed that they had not noticed the light that shone on them for a split second. We waited for what seemed an eternity for any movement or noise, anything prompting us to run or attack the two infected.

I faced my gun in the direction of the infected, preparing to fire upon them as I would shine my light on them again. I turned my flashlight on, hoping that they had remained stationary.

They had, but they were not alone. The flashlight illuminated a group of at least ten infected, all rearing to attack. I could see them as a pack of animals, their pale flesh contrasting the dried blood covering their bodies. They were disgusting to behold as they heaved silently in the ray of light. The foremost infected turned and let out a shriek that filled the entire facility as I screamed for the group to run.

I decided to make a run for the exit as we fired upon the infected. I could hear their hollow footsteps on the steel grating as we started to run forward. I focused my beam of light forward while I fired upon a nearby infected. Painful howls filled the air, reverberating off the metallic walls, signaling we had at least hit them with our fire.

As we began to run, the slit in the metallic exit seemed to be closing. It was getting smaller as we neared it, disappearing into nothing. I turned my beam at the base of the doors, wondering what was seeking to trap us in.

I was filled with anger as the light revealed an extremely large group of infected shutting the doors. We were so close to the exit that I could see their white demonic eyes looking back at me with satisfaction. I fired a few shots at them as I lashed out angrily with my words. We had to think of something quickly to help us get out of this situation. There was no way we could fight such an onslaught of infected.

My mind immediately flashed back to the map I had traced; there were a series of hallways that could take us back to the entrance, if we even had a chance of making it back. We were trapped; we had to try to make it back.

I pulled a flash grenade from my pack and tossed it at the infected before me. It went off as my group ducked into the hallway we needed to use to begin our journey backward. We ran through a series of hallways, chased closely behind by the shrill shrieks of the infected. We ended up in an arms room after another series of hallways; I felt some relief as I grabbed a few grenades and had my teammates grab whatever arms they could carry.

We moved to the far side of the room and stopped. The cries of the infected were beginning to fill the room we were in, and they were getting louder with every passing second. I pulled the pin out of one of the grenades and held the trigger patiently. I waited for a few seconds and then threw it into the middle of the room.

The room started to rumble as the infected were getting closer. The very bones in my body seemed to rattle at their oncoming presence. I smiled with utter contempt and malice as I saw the infected pour into the room. The grenade went off at just the right moment, and I reveled in every second of it. I saw them flying against the walls at the force of the explosion, with complete surprise on every one of their disgusting faces. We entered the hallway back as the room crumbled down behind us, burying those monsters.

Using various hallways and passing through other rooms, we were able to gather a few more supplies as we made our way back to the entrance. After making it back to the main pathway, I could see the entrance to the facility. I shone my flashlight on an extremely large pile of rubble behind us, forming a makeshift wall comprised of cement and steel. I turned to the entrance and proceeded on confidently. As soon as we had come upon the doors to leave, I turned to see another group of infected come pouring over the debris' edge. I grabbed another grenade, pulled the pin out, and threw it at the pile of debris.

We ran out across the empty plain as the explosion went off. We sprinted across the field, coming across the chain fences as some infected pursued us. We turned and fired upon them as they funneled into the gates. We killed all of them using our weapons and watched as the bodies piled up.

Then all was silent; I waited to hear more shrill cries fill the air, but none came. We turned back in the direction of the base, making the journey homeward. We traveled back through the night and ended up back at the base just after dawn. As soon as we got back, we debriefed the red haired woman's father outside of the house, relating everything that had happened.

After hearing us out, he scratched the growing white stubble on his chin as he thought on everything he had heard. After taking some time to think, he told all of us never to mention this mission to anyone. He asked for the sketches I had, which I gave up to him. I saw him look them over, fold them in half, and stuff them into his pocket. He said we would only use that route if we were beyond ourselves and were desperate enough to use it. Until then, no one would know what had happened. We all agreed to keep the mission a secret, never speaking of it again.

After remembering all that happened during that operation and all that happened during the attack last night, I looked into the faces of the other seven men that had gone with me.

The decision seemed unanimous as I looked into each individual's eyes. Each one of those men nodded as they could see what I was thinking. After seeing the unwavering faith in each of their eyes, I knew the next course of action.

I called out for silence as I waited to tell them what we were going to do. All eyes were on me, anxiously waiting for the final decision. Everyone gasped in complete shock as I called out, "We're going through the blockade."

TAPE #13

I was met with a largely negative response; many called out how that was a stupid idea that only sought the death of everyone on the base. Some said they would rather die in the house, making the infected come to us rather than going out to find them in order to die.

I listened half-heartedly at their remarks and outcries. It took a few minutes to calm everyone enough to let me speak. When they were ready to listen I told them, "Look, we have no other options. If we don't do something drastic we'll all die of starvation, or worse, at the hands of the infected. Would you really rather die here, helpless against the infected, when you had the chance to survive? That's so selfish! We're supposed to be trying to live! If we die like that, we may as well walk out there and offer them our necks because the infected will have already won! I know it sounds crazy, hell, I even think it's a little crazy! But it's something we have to try. Please, trust me. It's the only option we have left."

Immediately, a man cried out, "How would you know that this could even work? Nobody's been to the blockade since the outbreak. It could all be rubble, making a deathtrap for all of us to walk into."

That stumped me. I had just asked them to trust me, but I could not say that I had been there before. The trouble of politics weighed on me as I tried to think of a response. I got ready to give a confession, relaying the operation that had been conducted in detail. As I opened my mouth, ready to speak, one of the seven men spoke out, "I've been there! I know we can do it."

The crowd parted, forming a ring around him as he stood alone in the middle. He nodded at me, signaling for me to remain anonymous. He continued on, "I conducted an investigation under our previous leader with six other men. We made it through the blockade and its main complex and returned with some resistance from infected. It would be difficult, but not impossible. If this is our final option over dying where we stand, I say we go for it."

As soon as he said this, the other six men from the mission began to come forward, affirming his words. The group of seven men was set apart in the middle, understanding that I had to be anonymous for this to work. True, it was not as picture perfect as they told it, but it had to be in order for us to get the people on our side.

I felt guilty standing there, pretending not to know, but I knew it was for the best. I called out, "I leave it up to the majority vote: we either make a last stand here or try to make it through the blockade."

The vote was close. Many were in favor of staying where we were, but the group of seven men won the vote in favor of going through the blockade. I said, "It's been decided. We're going through the blockade. Everyone get ready because we leave in three days."

After the fate of our family had been decided, I began to assign the necessary responsibilities in preparation for our departure. We needed to gather all of our food supplies and arms; we needed to make sure we were ready for anything that might come our way.

Some came forward, asking the group what lie beyond the blockade. They said that it was a large forest, but there was no doubt that a town could not be far off. That gave some hope, enabling people to support the cause of leaving in the hope of survival. One skeptic asked for proof that they had been there. The men were able to point out the guns and other things we had brought back, but it did not satisfy her. I noticed that the red haired woman stood nearby, attempting to eavesdrop on the conversation.

One of the men spoke up about the drawings that I had taken, claiming them as his own of course, and how the red haired woman's father had taken them. The red haired woman turned and came right up to him. She said, "I think I've seen them. My dad had a couple of drawings that he would take out from time to time. Whenever I would ask about them, he would tell me that they were gibberish and none of my concern. That wasn't like him at all: he always included me in everything. One day, I got a good look at them. They looked like a series of pictures depicting some sort of floor plans. He always put them in a different hiding place."

I asked her if she knew where they were now, but she didn't. However, she went up to his room to look for them. As she looked for them, I continued delegating tasks while also making preparations of my own. I sent my little girl to pack her things and get ready while I prepared the larger tasks that needed to be done. The red haired woman came back about half an hour later, plans in hand.

I called the group of seven together alongside myself, the red haired woman, and a few others that could help lead to look at the plans. We arranged the faded drawings in order, constructing the floor plan of the complex.

The group that had gone was able to point out the access points that we could use to make our way through, avoiding as many infected as possible. They pointed out the areas where the debris was blocking the way and we would have to use hallways to get around. When they pointed out the room I had blown up with a grenade as an unusable route, I blushed a little bit.

We spent quite a while going over the plans and making sure we all understood how everything was structured according to how we would proceed through the complex. After going through that critical part of preparation, we dispersed, beginning the other final preparations that needed to be undertaken.

The first two days of preparation went smoothly, allowing everyone to leave behind anything not necessary for survival. We decided to have a sort of final supper on the third night, saying a farewell to those we had lost, the base we had called home for so long, and also taking time to have hope in our future.

Around midday on the final day, we were all set to go. Some

people had been delegated to prepare the meal, and everyone was ready to eat by the time it came around. As soon as it was ready, we were called in to wash up for our final supper.

As I was lingering behind to put some final touches together on the supplies we had prepared outside, my little girl came up to me, trying to pull me aside. When I asked her what was wrong, she told me that she couldn't tell me; all she could do was show me.

I grabbed her delicate hand as she pulled me into the house behind everyone else. She led me all the way back to our room; she really wanted to show me something. Once we had entered the room, she told me to sit down on the bed and close my eyes. I trustingly closed them, waiting for whatever surprise she would show me. I heard some shuffling and giggling as the girl crossed the room and returned to where I sat. She placed something in my hands and said, "Okay, open your eyes!"

I opened my eyes, looking down into my hands. It was a new picture she had drawn, but it was different from all the others. It was a picture of an ugly looking man in a pink and green jumpsuit. He had a victorious smile on his face as he was leaping through the sky. A bright trail of colors was following him, seeming to be propelling him through the sky. The sky surrounding him was light blue and filled with white puffy clouds. A smiling sun was in the right hand corner, encouraging the hero to fly higher. I instinctively turned the picture over, knowing I would see my little girl's signature, illegibly written, on the back. Instead of seeing what I had expected, I saw something that nearly tore my heart in two.

On the back of the paper, there was a note written in large letters. It read: "You'll always be my hero!" Underneath, my name was written in large pink and green letters.

"Why are you crying?" the little girl asked. At that moment I realized that tears were streaming down my face. They were hitting the picture, blurring the light blue sky and the clouds together. I looked up into her eyes, which were beginning to fill with tears. "You don't like it?" she asked in a cracked voice.

I immediately placed the drawing on the bed and wrapped the little girl in my arms. I whispered in her ear, "I love it. I absolutely love it."

I pulled the little girl back and let her stand in front of me again. We both began to wipe the streaming tears from our eyes as we laughed weakly. After a moment of collecting ourselves, the little girl gave me a big smile and said, "I made that for you. You can always remember that you're my hero and my bestest friend. I wanted you to have it before we leave the base tomorrow to go find a nicer place to be."

I thanked the girl again and almost began to cry for a second time. We heard the red haired woman's voice calling us down to dinner, our final supper. The little girl gave me a loving look and then bolted out the door in the direction of the stairs. I took a second longer to look at the drawing.

Tears began to well up in my eyes once again, landing on the paper and blurring more of the sky and its white clouds. I folded the picture into a smaller piece and tucked it into my pocket. More hot tears came down my face, landing in my open hands. I could see the moisture in my tears begin to cleanse my dirty hands, revealing streaks of my skin against the dark dirt.

My heart began to hurt, but I think it was a good hurting that time. It hurt in a pleasurable way, making me feel like I had gained something that was stitching its way into my body and filling the empty chasm of my heart. I sat there for a few more moments, reveling in that pleasurable pain. Then I collected myself, wiped my eyes, and headed downstairs for the last supper.

I don't really want to talk about what happened next, but I know I must. I can feel the tears welling up in my eyes as I get ready to tell this final part of the journey. Hold on, let me collect myself.................Okay, I think I can tell what happened.

It all started with the dream from before, a bad omen for sure. It had come and gone since it first started occurring, but this time it felt very real. I could feel every step and every second of it. I even felt the end, when I swallowed myself whole. There was only one difference: I did the swallowing; I was the monster in this one. Every other time I had been the one being eaten, but this time I was the one doing the eating.

I woke up in such a painful and frenzied state that I could no longer sleep that night. I got up and went to the chair by the window, watching the sky. It was completely covered in dark clouds, blanketing the sky overhead. I wished I could have seen the bright stars and moon I was used to, but all I found was the sprinkling of a heavy rain.

After trying to fall asleep for a while, I grabbed my backpack and my little girl's pack that were sitting by the door as I left the room. I decided to let her get some more sleep before we were to depart in a few hours. I carried the packs down to the front door and set them down.

I took a second to take a final look at the house. The streaks of blood had dried completely, becoming a natural part of it. The house was screaming out silently but painfully, making me nervous. I decided to go outside and watch the falling rain to help comfort me as I prepared to leave.

I opened the door to the covered porch and steps, taking in the fresh smell of the moisture in the air. I looked to my right and saw the red haired woman sitting down in a chair, her back against the wall. I walked over and sat in the chair next to her.

"It hasn't rained in such a long time around here that I forgot what rain was" she said, looking off into the distance. I agreed as I adjusted myself and sat back heavily in the chair. She looked over at me with a worried expression on her face.

"What?" I said, pretending not to know what she was thinking. "You had the dream again, didn't you?" she asked, already knowing the answer. I looked out into the distance, ashamed to meet her gaze. She continued on, "It's a dangerous dream, you know. You can't run from yourself forever." She paused for a second, and then said, "Was something different about it this time?"

I told her about it, and how I had been the monster this time. She said, "That's a bad sign. Something's wrong with you or with everything going on. You need to make sure you're careful today."

I nodded silently and started to watch the falling raindrops hitting the roof above us. The cloud cover spanning the sky made me uncomfortable, causing my injuries, past and recent, to ache slightly.

116

Maybe I was just getting old. We sat together in silence, listening to the world outside as we thought, until it came time for us to leave.

Everyone woke up promptly, ready to go. Some seemed hesitant to leave, and it was clearly evident by the anxious expressions on their faces. Others seemed confident and hopeful of what could lie on the other side of the blockade. Everyone had their supplies with them and waited for my final words before we parted. I saw the seven men from before at the front of the group, with my little girl, the red haired woman, and my little girl's "big sister" right behind. They all looked at me confidently, giving me courage and accepting my trust.

I began to give everyone my final address, saying, "I know by now that you've noticed it's raining. It hasn't rained in a very long time around here, so I guess it can be taken as a sign. What does rain do, really? It's a cleansing and growing agent that harbors life. Think about it: if it were raining inside, all of those blood stains on the walls would be washed away. Right now all of the blood on the outside is being cleansed, making our place new. It's also helping things grow. Every plant in the forest and field nearby is getting a nice long drink to quench its thirst. That will allow new life to spring from the ground and life will continue on.

I would ask that everyone here would let it rain in their hearts. I want all of us to be cleansed of our grief and pain while being quenched in order to grow. We can't do that here, in this house, which has seen so much death and bloodshed. I know every single one of you can hear the screams of the infected and our fallen friends as you pass through the halls and every room here. That's why we have to leave; we need to find a place where we can begin anew and grow, leaving the past behind.

I'm not saying to forget all that has happened; all I'm saying is that we need to leave to let these wounds finally close up. We don't need to remain here to remember those we have lost because we carry them in our minds and hearts every day. Take a second to look at the rain clouds covering the sky. They look gloomy, don't they? That's where we are now. But think about it this way; if we leave the dark covering above our heads, we will be able to find the sunshine we long for once again.

We have to leave now. We have to uproot our family from this place so we can find the sun once again. I was chosen to be your leader, and I think this is what's for the best. I'm asking you to trust me as I try to lead us somewhere new where a new chapter of our lives can begin........That's all I really had to say."

It was silent for some time after I finished speaking. I scanned the group before me; there were tears in their eyes. Everyone before me seemed to understand what I had been trying to say. I felt uncomfortable standing in front of them, waiting for some sort of response letting me know if they were behind me or not.

A woman who had lost her husband in the fighting during the surprise attack by the infected passed through the crowd and came up to me. She was a woman about my age; she looked older because of the time she had spent grieving for her husband over the past few days. She was a little bit shorter than me and had long blond hair. She had emerald green eyes that shone like jasmine, but they had begun to fade.

Losing someone who is supposed to be your other half and all that you have left of a life before the infection will do that to you. She had a dry, cracked face that housed a whimpering frown. She had long streaks of tears running down her face, meeting together at her chin, making rivulets that traveled down her neck. She stood in front of me for a moment, then threw her arms around my neck. She held me tight and whispered in my ear, "He would have trusted you, so I will too."

That made some hot tears begin to collect in my own eyes, but I managed to hold them back. She held me for a little longer, then let me go, standing there before me. I noticed that everyone else had surrounded us, bringing the whole family close. Many others began to come up to me, one by one with tears in their eyes, and tell me that they would trust me as I tried to lead them. It was an emotional time, giving me confidence as their leader as I began to weep alongside them.

After everyone had a chance to calm themselves, I came back in front of our family. There was no need for words as I looked into every one of their faces. I felt like I was going to cry again as I said, "Thank you so much. I will do my best for you and those we love. Let's go."

It took a little while for us to gather ourselves and belongings while knowing that we would never return to the house again. I made sure for everyone to double-check that they had everything and anything they absolutely needed. The rain outside was still sprinkling down, signifying that we still had time before the downpour began. After assuring ourselves we had all that we needed, those of us who could carry weapons grabbed them, and we headed outside.

The small droplets of water felt nice and cool on my face and arms as I walked out the door. I took in the view from the front of the house one last time; I could see over the brick wall, off into the horizon. The horizon was a blur of gray and green that day as heaven met earth in what seemed the far corner of the world. The forest grounded me, allowing me to see it in somewhat of its enormity. The gray in the sky seemed so meaningless that it looked as if the world had not finished being created, making the horizon the edge of the world where I could fall off at any moment.

I took a second to think about our orientation; we were a group of twenty-two that could move at a decent pace. The blockade, surprisingly, was only a day's journey northward at this pace, ensuring we would reach it at the peak of the storm's outbreak or any time after it had begun. I felt a small surge of confidence as I recalled it took my group half a day to reach it when we were sent on the mission to explore the blockade.

We came to the large steel gates of our base and slowly opened them, letting the world take complete form in front of us. The muddled image of gray and green welcomed us, beckoning us to leave the base we had called home for so long to step into the journey ahead of us. I looked back at the group and signaled for them to come on outside into the world before us. We looped around to the backside of the base, facing Northward in the direction of the blockade.

The rain that fell upon us was still a small sprinkle that refreshed me with every drop that landed on my dry and tired skin. We walked away from the base and into the forest, and I refused to look back. If I looked back at it, even despite all of its tragedy and pain, I could still see it as my home. If I looked back, I would have returned to it, never stepping into or attempting to complete this final mission through the blockade.

Greg Wilburn

I fought myself as I led the group into the forest as everything within me seemed to signal back in the Southern direction, right back into the arms of the base and its high walls. I eventually won myself out, holding on until the house was out of view and lost in the trees and the gray in the sky.

We made our way through the dense forest, which formed a dark green roof over our heads that protected us from the rain. I could hear the low pitter-patter of the rain hitting the leaves as I led the group on through the brush and trees. I felt anxious as I continued to face the fact that we were getting closer to the blockade, the final obstacle that would stand in the way of our new life.

I slowly remembered what I had seen on my previous visit there, and the anxiety began to increase with every step in that direction. I knew it would not be any sort of easy experience to try to survive that breeding ground for those monsters. We had made it sound so easy to accomplish when we told the others, but I and the other men knew the truth; it truly was a hell. There was nothing there but death and destruction. There was no way of telling how bad it had become over time, allowing the monsters to wait patiently for revenge upon us.

I tried to be hopeful in my mind, running through the plan we had formed using the diagram of the inside of the blockade. It seemed like a cake walk. However, I could feel the creatures' eyes on me, waiting for us to enter into their domain. We truly were going to the pit of hell and back this time.

I kept re-running the plan in my mind, giving myself some confidence that we were capable. I believed we were capable of getting through; I truly believed we would make it through and find the home we had always sought. We would have been home, our real home, away from all of the things we had suffered on this side of those walls. It sounded so unrealistic that there would be no difficulty over on the other side, but I had to believe that it truly was our perfect home. I had to believe and convince myself that this future was worth fighting and maybe even dying for.

If it wasn't, then there truly was no point or hope or purpose. It would mean that we were just fodder for the animals, doomed to live painfully until death came for us at the hands of the infected. I just had to believe, for my sake and the sake of all of those with me. I just had to.

I quietly led on as we continued on through the forest, passing brooks, streams, and an endless amount of trees. I tried to distract my increasing anxiety by listening carefully to the rustling of the leaves beneath my feet and the growing sound of the rain on the forest's roof. To no avail, my heart continued to sink into my chest, becoming a lead ball that weighed me down with every step closer to the blockade I got.

I could tell that it was beginning to get closer to dark as we went along because the shadows of the forest began to get longer and twisted, turning the serene forest into a creepy place full of gnarled and evil plants. The rain was getting harder as well, penetrating the roof above us and leaking in, hitting our backs. I was getting ready to have us stop for the night as the darkness began to descend even further.

Right when I was at the point of having us stop, it came into view. I could see the blockade off in the distance, at the top of a large hill with a big road leading right up to its entrance. It looked like a dark tower before us, standing in our way and preventing us from trespassing any further upon its territory. I lost myself in its evil for a second, realizing the fear that was beginning to cripple me, preventing any movement.

I came to when a hand grabbed my shoulder. I turned around quickly to meet the face of one of the men who had gone on the mission with me. I met his gaze as he said, "Should we stop here for the night? We need to rest up and be ready for this tomorrow." I nodded hollowly, consenting to his question.

He took charge in having us stop and set up a makeshift camp for the night. He had us take some of our materials to make a roof above us, protecting us from the rain. Those without weapons sat in the middle of our camp and watched all of our supplies that we had gathered alongside them, and those with weapons formed a circle around the camp to watch over everyone through the night. I finally began to contribute and set up various watches for the night, just in case any infected came around.

After setting up camp, we had a meal prepared. We ate a stew of potatoes, carrots, chicken, cabbage, corn, and peas. It was seasoned perfectly with salt, pepper, and a bit of paprika. Why I specifically remember the meal, I still don't know.

After eating heartily, everyone went to sleep as the dark fully penetrated the forest, allowing the entire world to become pitch black. There was no distinction from earth to sky as the rain clouds remained over us. It was all black, it was all evil. It seemed so foreboding as I sat there, trying to make out the blockade as my eyes adjusted to the dark around me.

I looked off into the darkness tiredly, and I knew I would not sleep that night. If I slept, the dream would come, and I felt that if I had to experience it one more time, it would break me. I listened to the sounds of the night: owls hooting, crickets singing, and the small whisper of the wind in my ear. I watched the night as the red haired woman slept on my shoulder, repeatedly waking up to check up on me and make sure I was faring well. I told her I was fine each time, and I could tell she didn't believe me for even half a second. Still, she left me to my worry, preparing herself for the day ahead.

We did not experience any trouble that night as we kept a vigil watch over ourselves, waiting for the dawn to greet us once again. I was the first one to see the morning light as the new day approached. Not only did the gray blanket in the sky begin to light up, but I saw the sun, even if it was for only a second.

There was a small tear in the sky's stitching, letting the sun's rays hit earth for a split second. Its rays landed before me, hitting the grass just outside of the forest's borders. It hit a small patch of grass, and the blades that were hit seemed to come alive in that short moment. They stopped their bend of depression and reached out for the sun, begging it to come down to them. They looked as if they were trying to uproot themselves as they desperately tried to reach the sun. I watched this phenomenon for as long as it endured.

As soon as the sun faded away into the clouds once again, the grass blades sunk low to the ground, even lower than the ones that had not gotten a chance to behold the sun. I studied and thought about that for a while, trying to understand what all that could mean. Maybe it was some sort of sign. Who knows? I kept thinking until the others started to awaken.

As the sky lit up, allowing me to distinguish between the gray sky and the depressed earth, everyone started to get up and prepare for our departure. We had a small breakfast of the leftover stew as we finished getting all of our supplies together.

As soon as we were all set and gathered, I came before them and told them, "Okay everybody, this is it. This is the last time we'll have to see any more of this place. On the other side of this place, just over that hill, is the place we will be able to call our true home. Make sure we all stick together and help each other through. Everyone will need to be quiet and careful as we proceed through the blockade."

I could see the nervousness in everyone; I could especially feel it in myself. I tried to suppress it as I continued on, "We've made it this far, and we're all going to make it through, every single one of us. We're a family, and family sticks together no matter what. Okay everyone, let's get going."

I led the procession behind me as we made our way up to the blockade's high walls. We came before them and walked alongside them until we came to a small entrance with a chain lined fence covered in barbed wire that acted as a doorway. On the other side was a small booth that had dried blood splattered all across its interior. I climbed over the wall next to it with another man and opened the doorway for everyone there.

I continued to lead the procession as we faced the series of chained fences that were laced with barbed wire all around. I saw bones wedged in between each pair of gates, revealing various infected that had most likely gotten trapped or killed there. The skeletons of the infected we had killed from the time before were not lying there in a pile, which worried me.

Still, I led us on through the series of gates and out into the open plain of wasteland. There seemed to be more bones scattered about the ground, which sparked my interest and my worry. I reached down before me and grabbed a nearby skull. It was covered in scratches and bite marks. I almost vomited when the answer hit me.

The infected were eating each other! I threw the skull down on the ground in disgust as I looked at the wasteland before me. Where I would see a graveyard of fallen souls they would see a buffet for the masses. Images began to take shape before me, and I saw the infected devouring each other and the bodies of their fallen brothers. How could such evil exist in the world? How could these demons do such a thing to each other? They truly were animals and devils that only sought to feed on their hate, each other, and us humans.

I looked over at the other men that were with me that night. They all had bones in their hands and were looking back at me. We all understood what had taken place over time as the humans ran out. We all looked at each other with pity and disgust; we were the only ones who knew, and we should be. No one else should know the diabolical nature of these devils. I led the procession through the open wasteland, past the remaining skeletons and the broken down cars up to the gates of the blockade.

To my surprise, the gates were wide open. They were the black gates of hell itself, clawing at us and trying to pull us into its hateful stomach. Those towering doors before us were smeared with dried blood, eagerly waiting there to paint themselves once again with ours. They were embodiments of evil, beckoning us to enter in each moment as we neared them.

We stopped before them, and the group patiently waited for me to make a move. I had such fear in my heart that I felt as if I were being torn apart by the very seams of my body. I tried to move, and felt as if I could only crawl. I cautiously stepped forward into the main entrance of the blockade, my descent into darkness. My feet echoed on the metallic floor of death, where I stopped and listened.

There was no sound; nothing at all. Even the silence was hiding from the unknown lurking there, from the evil that I could feel emanating from the very walls of the place. I could only smell destruction; it smelled of the chaos of death and war and evil all in one rank smell. I stood there, paralyzed, waiting for the darkness to consume me and never spit me back out. I could see before me, thanks to the tears in the ceiling which allowed the light of the gray sky to make its way into the blockade's interior and guide my eyes.

A voice came from behind me, asking, "Are you okay?" I stood there, unable to move. I watched as the red haired woman came before me, a concerned look on her face. I looked into her eyes for a second, regaining some strength and said, "Yeah, I was just thinking through the plan to get through this place." She clearly did not believe me, but she said, "Okay......perhaps we should get moving."

I agreed with her and turned around, facing the group. They were still waiting, eager to hear my command. I called them before me, beckoning them to enter. They walked in and stopped before me.

I took a second to take in the complex before me. There was a humongous pile of rubble before me, starting at the ground and reaching almost all the way to the roof. It was taller than I remembered, probable due to the grenade I had thrown last time. I looked to my right, where a room was mostly buried in debris and a service ladder had been torn apart; it led to a metal walk between the roof and the floor, creating a path past the rubble. But it was too far to reach.

On my left was the way we wanted to go. It was a small hallway that led to multiple others, eventually leading to a central room in the complex. I called the group of men from last time, the red haired woman, and a few others to me. We huddled together and went through our plan one last time.

We would take the first series of hallways to the central hub of the blockade, and then decide from there which way was the most effective option for getting us through the other half of the blockade. On the papers, we had determined there were four main hallways that led to other rooms and hallways, and each led to the other side of the blockade. At the very least we had four options. We had already determined that we would only split up if we absolutely had to, but we had to avoid that at all costs. After running through our plan of attack once more, we were ready to move.

I turned back to the group and had them begin to follow us through the first hallway. As we began to walk, I felt a small hand slip its way into mine. I looked to my left and found my little girl looking at me with a wide grin on her face.

"I want to go with you" she said in her beautiful voice that could move mountains. I clutched her hand and refused to let it go. Since she was with me, I had us walk behind the other men leading us through.

We passed through three or four hallways lit up a little by the light penetrating through the ceiling; the only sound we heard was the slow dripping of water and our heavy breathing. The sounds bounced off the walls made of stone and steel, filling the hallways before we could reach them. After those few hallways, everything went black.

The only light guiding us was the flashlights that some of us had, and they provided us with weak beams of light at that. The hallways seemed long and tedious to travel through, forming a maze that could be harboring danger at every turn. I used my flashlight to look at the plans of the complex, making sure we were on track with our plan and avoiding as many dead ends as possible. We seemed to be on course, with only a few more long halls to pass through.

We passed on slowly, letting the small lights projected by the flashlights guide us. We turned the final corner of the last hallway and found ourselves in the heart of the complex according to the floor plans.

It was a command center of sorts, completely fitted out with technology. There were computers everywhere, covering the floor and the ceiling. There were various consoles and desks covered in wires and rusted equipment. Even though all of the technology was probably out of date, it still felt new to me.

A spark of interest hit me as we began to scavenge the room, looking for any useful materials. What if we could find a computer that worked? Maybe we could get a message to someone for aid or at least to find out if anyone was even alive anymore. I scanned the consoles, passing over the ones with broken screens and missing parts. Most of the computers were broken or did not turn on when I pressed the power button. I went from computer to computer, praying to find just one that turned on. I had a few others join in the hunt, looking for a usable computer.

Some others in the room scavenged from the corpses around the room, calling out any items they could find, such as grenades or other weapons. I half-listened to these call-outs as we continued to look for anything to turn on. I came across a few computers that were smeared with blood on a console at the front of the room and pressed the power button. I pushed this one in, and nothing happened. I called out to the others helping me, asking if they had any luck. They all replied with hesitant no's.

I slammed my fist heavily on the keyboard with defeat. I turned and looked to my little girl, who was standing beside me. She looked up into my eyes hopefully and said, "it's okay, we can still get out of here. We don't need the computers." I looked into her eyes and smiled. I took her hand and began to walk away with her.

As we stepped away, a whirring sound began to fill the room. Everyone stopped and listened as the room groaned in the dense silence of the complex. We looked around with wonder, looking all around the room.

A spark of hope came into our hearts as some of the monitors came to life, lighting up the dense darkness of the room. I immediately called out for a person to get on every working computer, looking for anything that could help us get a message out to someone. I returned to one of the blood stained computers and began to slowly type in various commands into its system. It slowly responded, pulling up various tabs of information and operations. I quickly scanned through them, reading through various operations and protocols related to the outbreak so long ago.

Finally, I came across an emergency response system that had direct communications between the central complex and the military. This system fell under a tab called Shadow-Man. I stopped and called out to the others, asking if they could find anything that could open lines of communication with anyone. They tried for a while, but were unable to find anything. I called them over to me, to see if I had found anything viable. They crowded around me, looking at what I had found. I decided to send a message to the command, asking about the status of the outbreak.

We waited hesitantly around the computer for a response. After a few moments, a return message came back. My eyes grew wide with surprise as I read the message out loud. It read, "What is the status of your situation?"

I looked around as the others encouraged me to send another message about the situation of everything with us. I typed a message relating how horrible conditions had gotten in our area, the decrepit nature of the complex, and our plans to cross the other side of the blockade. I was patted on the back as we waited for another response, being told that the military would come and save us.

What bugs me the most is how everything fell apart with the next message. I am so angry that those who were supposed to help us turned on us, just like the infected. I am filled with contempt for them and what they did to send us into the jaws of death and end all of us.

The next message blipped onto the screen before us. I read it to myself and slammed my fists on the console in anger after. I turned to those around me as their hope faded. The red haired woman yelled out, "There's no way they can do this! It's murder! The bastards!"

A few of those waiting by the doors called out, asking what happened. I fell down to my knees as the alarms started to go off, filling the room with intolerable noise and flashing red lights. The message flashed before me, fueling a fire of anger inside of me. I read it once again, trying in some way to somewhat understand what they were thinking, sentencing us to death like that.

The message looked back at me, relaying the fact that the military had forsaken us by initiating operation Failsafe, which would shut down the complex on the side of the military, locking us into our side of the blockade and preventing us from reaching theirs.

The whole complex seemed to crumble as the operations took place. The procedure they were taking came up on the screen: they would let the steel-locked doors on their side go down, locking us in. Then they would bar up their side, locking the blockade completely. I stood up and began smashing the technology with my fists, my machete, chairs, and anything I could find. I screamed out amidst the wailing sirens, hating everyone and everything in that moment.

I went into a rage, destroying any piece of technology in my path. I don't know how long I did this, but I found myself against one of the cold stone walls, crying heavily as I pounded the floor with my fists.

The red haired woman came up to me, kicking me hard in the stomach. She pulled me up, yelling above the sirens, "Get up! We don't have time! We have to get the hell out of here!" I stopped myself and collected my gear. She pushed me forward, telling me to start sending out commands.

I began to take charge, sending a few to see if everything had been closed off ahead, and had some others begin to bar the doors on our side. They stacked desks, tables, computers, and whatever else they could find against our side, closing us off from the rest of the complex. A few minutes later, the men I had sent returned, verifying that steel doors were in the way of us and the next series of hallways, locking us in. I immediately had them begin to disable the sirens, stopping their annoying wailing so I could think. Dense silence filled the room again, and the leftover monitors provided us with some light.

I stationed men at both doors, just in case. I called some people to me so we could begin to form a plan. I looked over to the red haired woman, who was cradling my little girl in her arms as I spoke. We began to formulate various options, but we only came up with two: we could try to go back the way we came in, or we could try to find some sort of escape through the roof or some sort of service tunnel.

We started to look around on the floors and ceilings for any sort of hatch, and we found a panel that allowed access to the vents above us. First, we decided we would try to make our way back through the way we had come in. I called everyone in except those at the doors, relating our plan to them.

We immediately began preparing to depart, gathering everything together. I told the men who had built the makeshift wall barricading us into the room to tear it down. It came down with a large crash as tables and computer modules fell to the floor. As we prepared to leave the room, a rumbling sound began to slowly fill the room. I shushed everyone, waiting to hear the sound. It got louder with each passing second, almost as if a tidal wave was coming down upon us out of nowhere.

The red haired woman called out for the two men guarding the door to look into the hallway and check out the noise. The men picked up some flashlights and went into the darkened hallway. After a few seconds, the rumbling got low, crawling along the floors of the room. Then horrible screams filled the room over the sound of the rumbling, causing everyone in the room to panic. It could only be danger for us; I sent two other men after them, who hesitantly obeyed my orders and disappeared as well. I turned back to the others and told them, "We have to go through the vents; it's our only way out."The others unanimously agreed with me.

I grabbed a tall table and placed it right underneath the vent access door. I pulled the heavy steel slab off of the ceiling and threw it down on a nearby desk, breaking it and the computers that were on top. The loud crashing sound it made forced everyone to turn back towards the unguarded door, which remained dormant. I got down from the table and had another man take my place. I had him start pulling those with us up into the vents and make their way out of the room.

I grabbed a flashlight, unsheathed my machete, and called three other men to me. We had to see what had happened to the others who had disappeared. They grabbed their weapons and one other flashlight as we headed to the door. One of the men stopped me, telling me he would lead the way with the others and me stay behind them. I disagreed with him, but when the others told me the same thing, I passively accepted.

I turned around to look at everyone being lifted into the vents. I saw my little girl getting on the table with the red haired woman; both of them looked at me with worry, silently asking me if I would be okay. I nodded, affirming I would meet up with them again. I looked around at the base of the table; most of us had been sent into the vents to escape.

That gave me some peace as the small group with me prepared to search for the others we had lost. The men with me asked if I was ready as I turned back to face them. I consented and we made our way to the doorway.

When we reached the hallway, the low tone of the rumbling seemed to grab our feet, pulling us in the direction of those who had gone before us. One of the men shone the weak beam of light down the long hallway; it didn't even reach halfway. We looked at each other reluctantly, wondering if this was really a good idea. The lead man shrugged his shoulders and began walking into the darkness. The rest of us could do nothing but follow.

As soon as he had begun walking, the rumbling in the hallway began to increase in pitch and strength. It became more of a loud squeal as we stopped to listen. The hallway seemed to shake all around us as the sound increased quickly. Shrieks bounced off of the cold walls, sending a shiver down my spine, and preventing all of us from moving. The sound got louder and louder, ringing in our ears. I felt as if my brain were melting and leaking out of my head. All of a sudden, the sounds stopped.

The dark silence of the hallway stood in between us and whatever was lurking in the shadows. We waited, staring into the abyss before us, waiting for any movement or sound. Everything told me to run, not looking back, but I was glued to my spot, immobilized by curiosity and fear.

The silence was broken as we heard a tearing sound in the dark. It echoed in the silent hallway, amplifying its sound, making the tearing sound all the more horrible. Then it flew at us. It was an arm, a human arm. It landed hard, sliding across the floor and landing right in front of me. A trail of fresh blood led from my feet into the shadows of the hallway. The arm was in front of me, its hand still clenching and relaxing as it twitched on the floor. I felt vomit rising in my throat as I watched it move. The others stared at it, all of us not knowing what to do.

"All right" I whispered, "We have to get out of here. The others are dead." They all nodded in agreement, and we began to shuffle our feet back towards the control room. As we moved back, still facing the darkness, one of the men dropped his flashlight.

He juggled it in the air, trying to grasp it as it tried to flee. He wobbled it around, but it still escaped. It crashed loudly on the floor, sliding into the dark of the hallway. It came to a rest at the feet of the creatures of the complex, the dim light illuminating countless pairs of bloody, cracked, and gnarled feet. Blood was all over the floor, coating the feet of the sea of infected and the walls of the hallway.

I immediately turned and ran, the others following behind me. A thousand shrill cries filled the hallway as our footsteps led us back to the control room. The stampede followed us close behind, the sounds of thousands of feet clapping on the floor, an applause that caused a cold sweat to break out on my forehead.

We made it to the control room as the applause increased. We immediately turned and scrambled towards the table that stood underneath the open vent. I turned back to see the infected crash into the room. They were like wasps swarming out of their nest, covering everything in sight. They were disgusting to behold.

There were so many of them; women, children, and men that had become infected and were covered in blood flew at us. I let out a scream, ordering them to hurry into the vents. The first man leapt right up into the vent, extending his hand to pull me up. I grasped it tightly and jumped into the vent. We turned to help the others who had fallen a bit behind us. The scene that took place next still haunts me.

The man closest to us was halfway through the room as the last man was right in front of the tidal wave of infected. I screamed for them to hurry, seeing we had little chance to escape. The man in the vent next to me pulled out a grenade, getting ready to toss it into the room as we all escaped. As the man closest to us reached the table, the final man was caught by an infected at the ankle, tripping over a desk and landing hard on the ground. The two of us yelled out as they fell upon him, hungry to devour him.

The man at the table stopped short. He turned to see his friend being consumed by the monsters and lost it. He pulled out a pistol and began to fire upon the infected, leaving the table to encounter them head on. I can't remember what I screamed out as he left us to help his friend, but I remember that the man next to me prepared to throw the grenade into the room below us. I looked over at him and tackled him, trying to wrestle the grenade from him. He yelled out, "What the hell are you doing?! We have to kill them!" I screamed as I tried to take it from him, saying, "No! We can't! Stop! They're our friends!"

We continued to wrestle, but he got the upper hand. He got his legs underneath me and kicked me off of him. Then he jumped on me, punching me repeatedly in the face as I helplessly defended myself. He kicked me away from him and I hit the side of the vent. He turned, pulled the pin out of the grenade, and threw it hard towards the ground of the room below us. I dove at it, trying to catch it, but I just tipped it, causing it to land closer to the waves of infected filling the room.

The last thing I saw was the man who went back to help his friend. He was using a broken chair leg as a sword, fighting his way to his dead friend. The infected were attacking him from all sides, but he still managed to keep them at bay. He looked at us as the grenade landed right next to him. He gave us a wry smile, picked up the grenade, and dove into the midst of the infected, slashing as he went.

The grenade went off, filling the room with fire. The man in the vent pulled me away just in time to avoid the blast. He grabbed the collar of my shirt and looked me in the eyes. Tears were streaming down his cheeks as I looked at him. I could see how much it was hurting him to have done that. He said nothing for a second, then he threw me against the wall of the vent and said, "Let's go."

I silently followed as he went off in the direction of the others who left before. I put my hand to my face, seeing that I had tears on my face as well. We traveled along the length of the vents for some time, feeling our way through the dark, save the occasional streak of light that broke through the darkness. After moving through the vents for some time, we came across a giant gap in the venting system. There was a giant hole in the vent system, creating two sides in that space as a large abyss lie beneath us.

There was fire burning on both sides of the gap; someone must have let a grenade loose in the events. I kicked a piece of fiery metal down into the abyss to gauge how deep it was. It fell rapidly, completely disappearing from view.

That was it; we were stuck. The man with me and I began to plan, looking for any kind of solution. He looked up, pointing out some wires and cables that were dangling from the ceiling above us. I looked around, finding no other options. I looked back up at the wires; they did not look very sturdy, but it was still our only option. We climbed on top of the vent and clambered up the wall to get closer to the hanging wires.

Once we were close enough, both of us grabbed large handfuls of wires and prepared to jump. He stopped, telling me we should both go at the same time just in case the wires didn't hold. I agreed with him, and we began to count down from three.

We leapt from the wall at the same time, ripping all of the wires out of the ceiling as we crossed the gap. Sparks flew as he landed first, blinding me. I pulled my hand up to block my face, which caused me to lose grip on the wires I was holding. I hit my chest hard on the broken metal, which stabbed me directly in the chest. I let out a painful cry as I began to slip, lowering towards the open mouth of the abyss. The man with me caught me as I lost grip of the metal walls of the vents and fell. He strained to pull me up into the vent, pulling with all his might. He pulled me hard against the vents, the metal piercing and cutting my arms and chest.

Once I was up, we both sat back to catch our breath. I checked myself out, looking for wounds; I had a few deep cuts on my arms, which were bleeding slowly. I lifted my shirt, revealing two deep gashes in my chest with blood pouring out. I tore my shirt, creating a band that I tied tightly against my chest to slow the bleeding. The man asked if I was okay, and I said, "I'm a lot better than I would be if you had let me fall."

He let out a chuckle as he breathed heavily. We sat there for a second in silence, looking over at the other side of the vents. We could hear more shrill cries of the infected, and they were getting louder as they were following us into the vents. I looked over at the man and said we should probably get out of there. He nodded, and began to crawl off, me close behind.

We continued on in the vents, hoping we would find the others. We found some broken metal pipes that were pointed at the end as we went along; they would make perfect weapons. We kept moving in the dark vents, finally coming across a large room that I remember being close to the beginning of the complex.

We jumped out of the vent, landing in a large office room. It was quiet as we rummaged through the room, not finding anything useful. We left out of the left side of the room, going through a series of dimly lit hallways with various offices attached to them. I glanced through the broken windows as we passed, taking in the grim scenes of death, destruction, and decay.

We went on, finding another large office. We looked through this one as well, and the man with me happened to find a map of the complex hidden in a desk drawer. We studied the map, locating ourselves and realizing we were very close to the beginning of the blockade. I stopped to rest for a few minutes, feeling a bit lightheaded. I checked on my wounds again, making sure my torn shirt was even tighter across my chest. After resting for a bit, we continued on.

We walked through a few hallways, clamoring about in the darkness. We were coming upon another hallway when the sounds of gunshots filled the air. We instinctively dove to the ground, waiting for them to cease. When they didn't, we decided to go check out the situation.

We rounded the corner slowly, coming across some of those we had sent on ahead of us guarding the exit door of a large room. We entered the room from the right side, and across from us on the left side of the room was a crowd of infected coming through. They were being mowed down by the gunfire, creating a rising pile of carcasses in the middle of the room. We entered into full view of those shooting the infected and they saw us. They motioned us over while their yells were muffled in the gunfire.

The man and I made our way across the room, staying close to the walls on the right side. A few infected broke away from the others, coming straight at us. The man slashed two or three, incapacitating them. I killed one, and then allowed another to dive right into the metal rod as I shoved it into its chest. We kept out of the crossfire, reaching the men guarding the exit.

They motioned us down the hallway, yelling for us to help the others escape. Our thanks were lost in the sounds of the bullets as we left. We went down another dark hallway and turned into another. I collapsed as we turned the corner.

My vision went blurry and my head pounded as I fell to my knees on the ground. Bloody spittle was running out of my mouth, forming a puddle in front of me. I put my hand to my chest, feeling the blood that had soaked through my shirt. The man was helping me up, asking if I was all right. I could barely hear him over the sound of my pounding head. I assured him I was fine as I tried to walk on my own. I fell against the wall, trying to keep steady. He came alongside me and pulled me over his shoulder. He said, "You're sure as hell not all right" as he helped me walk along.

I laughed weakly as more bloody spittle fell from my mouth. My right hand still held tight to my metal rod, which was scraping loudly against the floor. I had him stop so I could look at the map; I needed to see how far we had to go to get the hell out of there.

The map gave me hope as I realized we were about to come to the entrance of the blockade. One longer hallway and we would be able to find the others, who had most likely gotten out of there and were making their way back to our base. I felt good that my little girl and the red haired woman had gotten out safe with the others. The prospect of them living gave me enough strength to begin to walk on my own as I led the way down the hallway to freedom. I could even see a dim light at the end of the hallway, which I assumed to be the light of the day outside. When I reached the end of the hallway, all of my hopes were gone.

The deceitful light at the end of the hall was just some light being let in through the high ceiling of the blockade. I fell to my knees again as I saw the doors to the entrance closed and sealed, with all of the others clawing at its entrance. They looked like trapped animals; fear was wide in their eyes as they desperately attacked the entrance doors. They were begging for anything to happen, for the doors to miraculously open. I saw a few watching the others with tears in their eyes; amongst them were my little girl and the red haired woman.

They were crying as they held each other, which tore my heart in two. I reached out to them, weakly calling their names as more blood fell from my mouth. They couldn't hear me; they were too focused on the sealed doors.

The man helped me up again, carrying me as I dragged my feet along the floor. I still refused to let go of my weapon; I clung to it for dear life. I studied the doors as we went over to them. They had most likely been shut earlier by the override the military had used; they had lied to us again.

The doors were barred across with large metal rods that extended across the entire span of the door frame. They were thick; way too thick to move even if we had an army. Anger rose with in me. They said they would only close their side. The bastards! Now we were all trapped with the infected biting at our backs. I called out to everyone as we reached them, trying to gain their attention.

The red haired woman was the first to completely face me; she held my little girl in her arms while holding a pistol in her left hand. Their eyes got wide as they saw me in my weakened state. The man with me threw his metal rod at the doors, which made a loud clanging sound that made everyone face us. Their eyes turned to us and got wide with worry as well. Some turned back and continued to try to unleash the steel bars more fervently as others flocked around the two of us.

My little girl came up to me while weeping; she hugged me tightly with all of her might, which made my whole body shake with pain. She said, "You're hurt! You're hurt! I'm scared! We're trapped in this place! We have to get out of here or else the monsters are going to eat us! Please don't die!"

I began to cry as the red haired woman approached, prying my little girl from me so I could breathe. My little girl wrestled in her arms, trying to get back to me. The red haired woman said that she was glad I was okay while fighting the little girl, an expression of complete grief on her face. I weakly remarked, "I've seen better days."

The others in the crowd came closer to us, desperately asking what we were supposed to do. I began to cry, putting a hand over my face as the tears came, as I admitted I didn't know. I sobbed, thinking of all the lives that would be slain here over my vain hope of getting out of there.

The man with me tried shaking me out of my despair, telling me that now was not the time to grieve; we still had time and life left. I agreed with him, trying to stop the tears that kept flowing down my face. I looked around the room as I sobered up, trying to find anything that could help us.

It was difficult as the crowd rushed me, begging me to hurry as they could hear the shrill cries of the infected emanating from the hall behind us. I saw a tear in the wall of the blockade where some light was shining through. It was high in the wall, near the top of the giant entrance doors. I could see the metal walk that extended near it to the giant pile of rubble that sealed us into that small space. If we could climb the rubble, then we had a chance. It was probably our only chance.

I turned back to the crowd, telling them what I could see. They looked at it, guessing it could work as our last ditch effort to escape. I had two men try it out to see if it could work. They struggled to climb the high pile of rubble, knocking large boulders down near us as they ascended. They made a jump to the metal walk and landed on the steel grating. They ran across it, moving to the tear in the wall. One of the men went through as the other waited.

After a few moments, the man waiting yelled down to us. The blockade had a steep slope to it, allowing the other man to slide down towards a drop-off, which kept him from climbing back up to where the tear was. He would have to wait outside. Knowing that the plan would work, we decided to give it a go.

As soon as I said it would work out loud, everything changed. A mad scramble broke out, starting with those who had been clawing at the doors. They turned towards the pile of rubble, sprinting right into those that had gathered, knocking most of us down as they stampeded through.

I was knocked to the ground, watching the feet fly over us, stepping on us. I watched as the red haired woman and my little girl fell, hitting the ground with thuds. I was kicked in the face and in the chest as they ran through, forcing me to scream out in agony. My vision blurred, going in and out as I watched those around me being trampled. I heard the cries of my little girl and red haired woman amidst the panic of those running over us. I heard a few wet snaps, which I believed were the breaking of bones.

As the group stampeded past and my vision cleared, I got on my stomach and dragged myself over to the others. I saw that my little girl was holding her leg, which was most definitely broken. The red haired woman sat up, holding her bloody face and her ribs. Various others around me had swollen bodies, trying to get to their knees. I looked to my left, where the man who had helped me was nursing a broken wrist.

I dragged myself over to the girls, stopping short as the rumbling started. I looked at the pile of rubble, which was giving way under all of the people rushing towards the high metal walk. The room began to shake as the rock broke away from itself, sending those on top plummeting back down towards us. I screamed for everyone to get clear of it as we tried to pull ourselves away from the falling rock. I jumped on top of the red haired woman and my little girl as the rocks came tumbling down.

I coughed as I opened my eyes. The light was illuminating the dust in the air, causing the dirt crystals to shine like stars as they danced in the light. I looked around as I called out if anyone could hear me. I heard a few muffled responses as I looked beneath me.

The red haired woman and my little girl were clutching onto me while they both cried. I tried to pull myself up, realizing that my feet were caught underneath some of the rubble. The girls got out from underneath me, nursing their injuries. The man who had helped me broke out from underneath some of the rubble, helping lift the rubble that covered my feet.

I looked up at the metal walk, where two men and one woman had joined the man waiting up there before. They called down to us, asking if we could make it up. I looked over at the pile of rubble that had fallen. Only half of it was standing, revealing a broken service ladder that led up to the metal walk. I yelled up to them, saying we would try to get up there using that ladder. They said they would wait there to help us up.

I had the man with us look for other survivors while we made our way up the rubble. The red haired woman stood up, taking my crying little girl up in her arms. She helped me stand, asking if I was strong enough to climb. I assured her I was, sending her ahead of me to climb. I began to climb up the rubble slowly as I felt my body growing even weaker. The wounds in my chest and arms were burning me up from the inside out, making me feel as though I had been set ablaze.

The man returned quickly after we had begun to ascend, coming up to me. I asked him again if there had been any other survivors, to which the watering eyes in his head told me more than I needed to know. I began to feel pain well up in my chest as I tried to envision what he had seen, and at the same time for all the lives that had been lost all because of me.

He saw it in my eyes; he looked at me and said, "It's not your fault...It's not." I tried to believe the words coming out of his mouth, but the burning pains in my heart were telling me otherwise. I nodded, lying to give him some comfort with what he had said. He came beside me, helping me up so we could climb. The girls were not far ahead of us as we climbed, and as the final flood came rushing in.

The evil cries of the infected filled the halls and the small expanse of the space we were trying to escape from. Everyone stopped, looking back as the tide came in. A large crowd of infected smashed into the room, covering the ground beneath us. They began to tear into the rubble, digging out the dead bodies of the others and beginning to feast.

I looked on in horror as blood rained down on the infected as they tore into the bodies, coating their pale skin with red. I cursed them with every word I could think of as they tore them apart, splitting them into pieces as a tearing sound filled the room alongside their cries. The man tried to drag me up the rubble as I tried to pull myself away in the direction of the infected to fight them all with the metal rod I still held tight in my hand. I screamed and kicked as I was dragged away, looking on with hate as bloody body parts and organs flew through the air.

As I cursed, I gained the attention of many of the infected. Fear crept down my spine as I saw many of them make eye contact with me, hungering for their next meal. My bravery ceased as I looked upon them, rearing up and getting ready to attack. I turned, allowing the man to help me up as their screams echoed in the room. I kept my eyes forward, seeing that the girls were not far from us at all; the red haired woman struggled to climb with my little girl clinging to her. I shouted for them to hurry, hearing the screams of the infected getting louder as they began to ascend the rubble.

The man and I moved over the rubble quickly, driven by fear. We sped over the rocks, kicking some down to slow down the creatures. We came alongside the girls and began to help them up the rubble. We inched closer to the broken ladder as the creatures came near. The man turned around, kicking the lead one square in the face. I turned and stabbed another in the face. Both tumbled down the rubble, taking some of the others down with them.

Now all of the infected were scaling the rubble, headed straight towards us. We turned and rapidly scaled the last of the rocks, reaching the service ladder. I sent the red haired woman up first as she was breathing hard. My little girl jumped out of her arms and into mine. Some bloody spittle was flowing from the side of the red haired woman's mouth as she looked at me with thanks. She climbed up as quickly as she could.

I turned my attention to my little girl, saying, "I need you to ride on my back. You can't let go no matter what, okay?" She nodded and then climbed onto my back, latching onto me with all of her strength. She wrapped her good leg around my torso, which burned a lot. The broken leg dangled freely in the open air. I handed my weapon to the man and began to climb. I looked down to see the man right behind me, fending off as many infected as possible.

I continued to climb, trying not to let go as my head throbbed and my vision began to go in and out. My chest was pounding hard, feeling as though it would burst at any given second. I reached the metal walk and had just ascended to it when I lost everything......

I looked down to see the man overcome by an infected, fending it off with the metal bar. As he fought, another infected leaped from the one fighting the man, using it as a step to leap to the metal walk. It landed in front of me, rearing up for an attack.

I will never forget that infected; I hope it burns in hell for what it did. I remember it exactly: it was a larger infected, covered in faded tattoos. It was wearing bloody jeans and a torn shirt. On its left arm was a tattoo of the grim reaper nailed to a cross with a scythe through his head. The inscription underneath read: "I've killed Death; what can you do to me?"

Its forearms and hands were tattooed over with vines covered in thorns. Blood was dripping from each of the thorns. Its left leg had a tribal design that went from its thigh down to its ankle, and through its torn shirt I could see flames tattooed on its chest.

A few long strands of white hair were clinging to its scalp. Open wounds covered its body, and each one was oozing. Its cloud white eyes revealed small black veins reaching for irises that were no longer there. Its nails were long, gnarled, and were dripping blood. It seemed to smirk as green spittle flowed from its red mouth.

It stood before me, breathing heavily. It stood towering over me, causing a sweat to break out over my shaking body. I told my little girl to go over to the others, and she limped quickly away as I bent down to let her go. I turned back to the infected and took a step back as my courage left, stepping into two other men on the metal walk, who were standing behind me.

I looked past them, seeing the women and one of the men standing by the tear in the wall. I turned back to face the behemoth, gaining courage as my friends stood with me. The creature leaped forward as the three of us charged him.

He kicked one of the men in the chest, causing him to fly into the others by the tear in the wall. He grabbed the other and smashed him into the wall face first. I saw an opportune moment and tackled him hard in the stomach, sending us towards the edge of the metal walk. I punched it in the face hard as it seemed to laugh shrilly. It grabbed my throat and lifted me high into the air as it got out from underneath me. I gasped for air as it held me suspended over the edge of the walk.

It all happened in slow-motion as I watched my little girl tear herself away from the others and limp rapidly over to us. I couldn't scream for her to stop as I gasped for air. She came right up to the infected, latching onto its leg and clawing at it. The infected turned its attention to her for a split second, giving me the chance to raise my legs to my chest and kick it hard in the throat. It released me as it hit the wall of the blockade hard, holding its throat.

I was suspended in the air for a second before I latched onto the edge of the metal walk. I had both hands clutching onto it with all of my strength. My little girl came up to me, trying to pull me up onto the walk to no avail. I looked over her head to see the infected regain its breath and begin to walk over to us. I screamed for my little girl to run, but she would not leave me. I began to curse her, yelling for her to leave me at all costs. The infected kept coming closer, extending its hands towards us, which was all the more horrible as I watched in slow-motion. As it came up to us, the red haired woman flew into it, knocking it over the edge. I watched in horror as it latched onto the leg of my little girl, taking her with it.

I screamed as I instinctively wrapped my legs around her, holding her with everything within me. My grip was fading fast as I looked down, seeing that the infected was clinging onto her leg. The red haired woman, the other woman, and the men came to me, trying to keep me from letting go. I howled in pain as I could feel my arms tearing themselves from my body; I was being ripped at the seams as I held the weight of both my little girl and the infected.

My little girl was clutching my stomach as she screamed for help, but none would come. I looked up with helplessness at them, yelling for them to do something as I began to slip. They took off their shoes and threw them down at the infected, trying to make it release its grip.

One of them hit my little girl in the hand, causing her grip to slip as she began to slide from in between my legs. I looked down, seeing the infected swing its arm and grab the broken leg of my little girl. Her cry filled the entire space, causing me to cry out angrily as I remained helpless. Her screams pierced my ears and my heart as the infected tugged at her. Her grip began to slip as she began to slowly slide away from me. I screamed at her, yelling, "Don't let go! Don't let go! Don't let go! Don't let go!"

Tears flew down my face as I felt my arms separating from my body. The infected cried out as it pulled even harder on my little girls' legs. Her screams were killing me as her grip slipped again.

My legs were beginning to ache and shake all over as I held onto her with all the strength I could muster. I yelled out in utter agony as my arms separated from my body, the sounds of the dislocations filling my ears. The only thing holding me up was the five of them on the metal walk.

The infected pulled even harder on my little girl, and I heard the loud pop of her legs as they separated from her body. She let go in that moment as I looked down.

My legs reached out to try to grab her one last time as I saw the two of them fall towards the ground far below us. I screamed as my heart shattered in my chest and as the others pulled me up onto the metal walk. I could not move as I cursed them. I cursed everyone and everything as they dragged me away and slid me out of the tear in the wall of the blockade.

The light of the sun blinded me as I entered the air outside. I screamed and cried and kicked and cursed as we went down, landing hard on the ground in front of the blockade.

I tried to get up, to go back in and try to save my little girl. I knew it was too late, but I could not let it go. I had to go back in. She needed me. I made her a promise. I had to keep it no matter what.

I couldn't get past my knees as pain surged through my body. I continued to scream and cry and kick as the others came down, coming alongside me and dragging me back in the direction of the base we had left.

The man who had helped me managed to escape fighting the infected. I saw him pull the pin to a grenade and throw it into the blockade behind him as he leapt down and slid to us.

They dragged me away into the distance as the explosion filled the air. I saw the flames well up, spitting a few infected bodies out onto the ground. I cried out in protest as they continued to drag me away from that place. I cursed them, I cursed the infected, I cursed everything, I cursed myself for losing everyone, and most of all, I cursed myself for losing her.

I broke my promise to her; I broke the only promise I had to keep. I screamed until my voice was hoarse and I kicked until the pain would not let me move any more.

TAPE #14

And now I find myself here, back at the base we should have abandoned forever, which can never truly be a place of any hope to me after all that has happened. It's all been desecrated and destroyed; it's all over. We lost.

I'm sitting in my room, in the chair looking out into the clouded sky. When I look at the walls around me, all I can see are the mistakes I've made and the failures I have become.

My little girl..........I see the art she spent so much time making. It's happiness amidst the evil that constantly surrounded and tried to devour her, brains and all.

The drawing of me as her hero is my favorite.......I'm looking at it now and hating every second of it. It has some blood on it, on the upper left corner of the page. The dried and smeared droplets look as if they are trying to infect the page as the once white clouds have started turning red and pink.

At the same time, this infection seems to be trying to infect the beautiful hands that made it, tainting all I have left of my little girl in my heart, which makes me so angry at everything that happened and especially at myself.

I'm trying to ignore that as I take this long look at the picture. I can see the hero in the middle; even though the face is all wrong and he has a pink and green jumpsuit, I still love it. It lets me know she thought I was a good guy despite all the wrong I've done. I hope she could still believe that if she were here with me now.

It makes me believe that I still have a chance to be good even though I only see myself as evil; I am stuck wondering if I truly have become the monster, devouring myself from the inside out until nothing of me is left.

It's only me, the red haired woman, another woman, and five men left. We have three guns with little ammo, some forgotten food supplies, and some melee weapons. We really have nothing; the infected have won. We all know it.

They followed us back here, lurking in the shadows of the forest. Their shrieks fill the air around us and seem to get closer with each passing minute. I don't want to make any sort of last stand; there's no point.

The red haired woman told me a secret: she found this recorder and various empty tapes a while ago, and she would document her life on some of them in order to tell her story to others in the future. She has given all of it to me now because she says I need to talk; I need to give presence to the pain that is devouring me from the inside out.

I honestly think it's stupid, but it kills some biding time and she says that it is the only way to combat it. She says that someone needs to know; they need to hear what real life was like from a guy like me.

Why me? I'm nobody. I'm just a guy who went from being nothing to being less than that as everything was ripped from him, leaving him an empty shell of his former self.

This is the final tape left, and........I guess this is the end of my story. I pray that someone finds it. I pray that it can make the difference I never could.

This is the end of me and all that I am. I hope it's just your beginning.........

(end tape)

BOOK/AUTHOR UPDATES AND INFORMATION:

www.darkdaysinfectedbook.webs.com
www.facebook.com/darkdaysinfected

Contact Us:

(949) 287 - 3106
www.darkdaysinfectedbook.webs.com/contact-us

Greg Wilburn

ABOUT THE AUTHOR

Greg Wilburn is a college student living in beautiful Southern California with his mother, sister, and brother. He hopes one day to become an English teacher.